Selena's Magica Somnia

Book 1: *The Witch of the Crescent Moon*

A.V. Dawn

LWP

Dedicated to the love of my life, Taylor

With you I feel like I am walking among stars and basking in their splendor. You have shown me there are still many beautiful things to discover along my journey through life, and I am grateful for the lesson. Thank you for sharing your magic with me and bringing color back to my world.

I.

Sigil of the Full Moon

Often I dream of a cold night by the shore of a still lake, the moon clearer than ever reflected across its dark waters. At the water's edge, there is a woman with a large snow-white witch's hat and a white fur cloak. There is an ethereal quality to her as she stands draped in a pale blue, ombre dress that grows dark and sparkles like the night sky at its hem. She stares into the lake, bluish-black hair cascading down her back and her bare toes dipping into the water.

Then she looks back at me with her crystal blue eyes, and raises her left hand, revealing a strange image—an orb representing the moon, surrounded with a ring, and from that ring are lines curving out to form a snowflake pattern.

It is the Sigil of the Full Moon, though I don't know how I know that.

A slight smirk creeps across her frosty pale face.

I wake from my dream with my head in a fog, sitting up in my big, empty bed and looking around blankly, the dark blue comforter falling to my waist. It takes me a minute to register the irritating sound of ringing and beeping that make up my phone's alarm.

I search the dark covers for the offending device until I finally feel the cool plastic of its galaxy-purple-patterned case against my fingertips. I pick it up and silence the blaring alarm, restoring my phone's usual stock space background.

As always, waking from that dream leaves me exhausted and drained. The choice to either get up or fall back asleep makes itself for me as the weight of my head draws me back to my pillows. My eyes seal shut, and it takes two more alarms before I drag myself free of my bed's warm, dark embrace.

I shower and dress for school, figuring jeans and a purple hoodie will be fashionable enough for a Monday morning. I run a brush through my long, black hair just to get the knots out, and I'm ready to go. It's too early and I'm too tired to care about impressing anyone, anyways. My only concern is staying comfortable walking in the morning chill. My skinny frame is quite vulnerable to the cold.

The weather always changes so fast in September. At the start of the month, it feels warm enough to keep the air conditioning on, but by the last week, it would be cold enough for a winter coat if not for the sun's warmth.

Still, I am one of those rare sorts who like the winter. My whole family likes it cold—my dad's rough stubble develops into a small, soft beard, my mom pulls her long hair back into a ponytail and wears the most beautiful winter fashions, and I always find it more comfortable to be a little cold than a little hot.

As I meander through the cream-colored hall of my house, my black socks slippery against the hardwood floors, I can hear Dad downstairs humming some vaguely familiar song to himself. Whatever he listens to in the car invariably becomes the following morning's performance.

I sigh as I drag myself down the creaky L-shaped staircase. I can predict what he will say verbatim, mouthing along the words as I cross the threshold between the stairs and the front door to slip on my black running shoes.

"Selena," he calls as I silently mock in tandem, "you should eat something before you go, you'll focus better in class with a full tummy!"

I keep his tall, pudgy frame in the corner of my vision and roll my eyes as I slip on my shoes without untying them, my weathered black backpack slung over my right shoulder. I definitely look more like mom than him, even if we do have the same eyes.

"Bye, Selena!" he calls, the morning sun reflecting off of his glasses and obscuring his blue eyes. "I love you."

As I open the door Dad calls again, playfully impatient this time: "I said I love you!"

"Oh my God, I love you too," I whine with a scowl, closing the door and walking around our plain, patchy lawn and our boring blue hatchback to the sidewalk.

I pay little attention to my surroundings as I navigate the sidewalks. I always found suburbia to be stifling, with endless arrays of the same houses arranged in neat little grids, broken up by the occasional park or plaza. Uniformity feels like the death of creativity to me, and, indeed, there is little imagination on display here. The most unique features to be found is an occasional flower bed or fancy glasswork on a front door.

Finally, I find myself outside of a square-shaped, three-story building: my high school. It is almost perfectly symmetrical, except for the extended rectangle that made up the gymnasium jutting out from the right side and running the length of the building. Crowds of kids from fourteen to eighteen file into the building like a haphazard cloud of dread—I imagine very few are here because they want to be.

Surrounding the property and separating the parking lot from the school grounds is an eight-foot-high white wall, and by the iron-wrought gates that lazily hang open stands Cara with her long ginger curls and a verdant sweater, a white skirt hanging down to her knees with black leggings underneath.

She smiles at me and waves enthusiastically, eliciting my own meek one in return. "Selena!"

Cara is always so expressive. She smiles wide with large dimples, flashing her white teeth every time, and her big green saucer-eyes twinkle behind her large, round glasses. She emits a radiating positivity that is hard to dislike, even if it does fill me with second-hand embarrassment.

"Hey, sorry I didn't make it to book club," I say as we start to walk inside together. "I was really tired Friday."

"That's okay! I'll catch you up later. And, speaking of clubs, I joined a new one!" she says, practically bouncing on her heels as she waits for me to give her the chance to explain further.

"Another one? You're in so many, on top of your archery practice."

"This one is cool, it's the anime club! Every year they make all these cool cosplay outfits, they're going to teach me how to sew and stuff."

It seems like every week or so that Cara picks up a new interest. In some ways, it's a little exhausting to keep up with her, but in other ways, I'm a little jealous. I've never felt that kind of passion for anything.

I find myself drifting through the school day like always, mustering just enough attention to keep my grades up, but otherwise finding it all boring. I feel out of place, in a sense, like I'm here because I don't know where I should be instead.

We have gym class last period, and today the teacher has us out on the football field. Having forgotten my outdoor running shoes, I sit this class out after doing our warm-up stretches, retreating to the bleachers with several other forgetful classmates to watch Cara and the others run laps then play soccer. My mind wanders as they play. Though I don't know much about sports, I have to assume that a football field would not pass as a FIFA-approved soccer field. Are soccer fields and football fields the same size? I look it up on my phone, and Google is quick to tell me that in fact, soccer fields are much wider. I suppose that must be nice for Cara and the others since they don't have to run as much.

I look up at the sky and notice the moon is visible today. It's mesmerizing, and it becomes more and more clear as

I stare at it, an enchanting crescent that I cannot look away from.

I blink—

And now I'm alone in the dark.

It feels like the middle of the night. How long was I staring at the moon? A moment? Or hours? Am I asleep?

A strange hypnotic compulsion drives me to climb down the bleachers, but when I reach the bottom, I am instead on the sidewalk at an intersection of two streets which stands at the border between suburbia and a dense, endless forest. There's a chill in the air and the wind penetrates me to my very bones.

My vision feels fuzzy, and I find myself struggling to focus on details, but the street signs stand out clear as can be. Owl Street and Fantasia Circle.

Thoughtlessly, I step toward the woods that run the length of Owl Street, away from suburbia, and I am suddenly at the edge of a long driveway cutting through the woods. The leaves loudly rustle all around me as I follow the winding path, almost drowning out the echo of the gravel crunching beneath my feet. It's like the sleeping forest is waking up to announce my arrival. At the trail's end I find a secluded, gothic-style black and white house on a hill with a pond and a large yew tree out front.

I am unwittingly transported once more, this time to the library inside the house, a large two-story room with a big, open area in front of a massive bay window that overlooks a garden. A green moth flutters just outside.

Painted on the floor in the library's center, illuminated by moonlight, is the Sigil of the Full Moon.

Outside the window, beyond the garden, is the lake from my dream, the moon looming large over it. The gentle sound of the water stirring against the shore fills my ears. Something about it calls to me, and everything else blurs from my vision. I step towards it, but as my foot touches the black paint I wake from my stupor, back on the bleachers, with the sun shining in my eyes.

I can feel my heart pounding as if trying to leap from my chest, and I struggle to find my breath. I look around and everything seems normal. When I look up the moon is no longer visible.

Was that a dream? I feel an alien sense of motivation, as if something buried deep inside has just woken up.

I check the skies for the moon once more, but it's not there. Then a thought occurs to me. I check the maps app on my phone, and sure enough, the intersection I saw is real, and not far from my house. And just from scrolling around the map, I can see that Owl Street has a few large manors just beyond the trees, and one, the one with the longest driveway, looks like it might be the one I saw—and just beyond that house is a large lake called 'Falling Star Lake'.

"Hey, Selena!" Cara calls, alerting me to class coming to an end. "Are you okay?"

"Yeah, I just had a weird moment, that's all," I say, faking a small smile.

Her big eyes see right through me. She's clearly skeptical, judging by her squinting and the way she scrunches up her nose. "What kind of a weird moment?"

"I don't know, I guess I just felt something, that's all. It's probably just in my head."

"In your head is where you live! Talk to me, bestie."

I sigh, then show her my phone. "I had a daydream or a vision or something of this house ... I feel like a crazy person, but I don't know, maybe it means something?"

"Okay, well, first of all, we don't say 'crazy' because that's insensitive, and you are not allowed to put yourself down," she lectures, eliciting an eye roll and a smile from me, both involuntary. "And second of all, if you think this means something, then let's go there and see! What's the harm?"

"I guess?"

We hear the bell ring in the distance, so I text my parents *'Hanging out w/ Cara for a bit, be home for dinner, luv you'* and we go change and collect our things from our lockers.

The path to Owl Street feels familiar as we walk—even without the help of the maps app, I feel like I know exactly where to go. Sure enough, I find myself approaching the intersection from my dream, passing it, and eventually coming to the long, winding driveway.

I stop at the edge of the property, and, again, that familiar thumping in my chest returns.

"What is it?" Cara asks.

"It's just like what I saw."

I walk up the path, just like before, but with Cara at my side this time. I see the yew tree from before, its branches hanging over the small, round pond. And at the foot of the tree stands a man, taller by a head than any other I've seen, with shaggy brown hair halfway down his back and a full beard.

Upon his left hand is the Sigil of the Full Moon.

He turns away from the tree and looks at us with apprehension on his worn, weathered face; his left eye is brown, almost amber, and his right is a pale, frosty blue. He reminds me of a wild old dog, yet, somehow, I know I don't need to fear him.

I take a step forward and take a deep breath.

"Who are you?"

II.

The Wolf

The man looks back at Cara and I incredulously.

"Who am I? This is my property, who are you?" he barks back with an irritated scowl. "I put up a no soliciting sign for a reason, girl scout."

Cara confidently steps forward. "Okay, I feel like you are using the word girl scout as a pejorative and that is a microaggression, so if we could try again–"

"Get off my property!"

"Your tattoo," I say, ignoring him. "What is that symbol?"

The man immediately takes a heavy step forward and his face becomes flush with anger. "What's it to you?"

I feel a sense of budding wonder and curiosity as I step closer. It feels as though this is the moment I've been waiting for, even if I never realized it. "I've seen it before."

"I doubt that," he says, turning away from us and walking toward the house.

"I saw it in my dreams! There's a lake, and it's dark out, and there's a full moon, and there's a woman with dark hair there." He stops dead in his tracks. "The woman has that same tattoo in the same place. It means something."

"It's just a tattoo. Now get lost," he commands wearily as he goes back inside his house.

Cara and I walk away in silence. The lake from my dream comes to mind, and my eyes dart behind the house, to where the app said Falling Star Lake should sit. I wonder if they really are the same, and what it means. Going back now would definitely be considered trespassing, but at the same time, I just have to know.

"How come you didn't tell me about that dream?" Cara asks, glancing at me from the corner of her eye.

"I thought it was just a weird dream until today, but now it feels like something more," I say, stopping in the middle of the path. "There's supposed to be a lake back there, it's the last thing from my dream and I just have to see it, would you come meet me here tonight after dark?"

"Why after dark?"

Because it won't resemble my dream in the day. "So he can't see us."

Just like we agreed, Cara meets me back at the spot halfway along the driveway at ten in the evening, both of us in black hoodies and yoga pants. She carries a long, narrow black case on her back.

As we trudge through fallen leaves and muck I'm grateful for Cara. No one else would come trespassing on some stranger's property in order to find out if my dream has any meaning—but Cara is that kind of friend. I know she doesn't believe in anything spiritual, and yet here she is, without question. I have never once worried that she would be anything but supportive.

Even with the light of our phones, it's tough. We are constantly tripping over roots, bumping into branches we can't see, and struggling on uneven ground, while the rustling of the trees and the sounds of the woods have us looking over our shoulders and jumping at every odd shape and shadow. But, eventually, light starts to peer through the trees, and the foliage starts to thin. We emerge on a dirt path that leads from the garden behind the big house to the shore of a still lake. We turn our lights off and I step toward the lake in awe.

It's just like my dream. The crescent moon sits in the sky, reflected perfectly on the water's surface, the same gentle chill in the air—all that's missing is the woman in the white hat at the water's edge.

"I've been seeing this exact image in my dreams off and on for years . . ."

I step toward the shore, and as I do, I notice the one thing out of place here. A waist-high stone cairn sits just at the edge of the water, where the woman would normally be standing.

I approach it in a trance, everything else in my field of vision becoming blurry. There is just the cairn, almost opaline in the moonlight, and the space between it and me. I reach out, but just as I am about to touch it, I hesitate. A sense of uncertainty fills the logical part of my mind, even as something inside me pushes me to continue.

Suddenly, the woman from my dreams is beside me—or an apparition of her. She is luminescent and ethereal, a glowing haze standing right before me.

Gently, she holds my wrist and guides my hand to the cairn, and as I press my fingers against the cool stone, a wave of blue light flashes across the rocks.

The woman disappears as the cairn collapses in on itself, turning into a pile of unassuming rock.

"She's gone!"

"Who?" Cara asks.

"The woman, she was right here," I say, gesturing.

Cara looks back at me apprehensively. "I didn't see any . . . one . . ." Her voice trails off and her pupils expand, and I can see her begin to tremble.

I turn around to see a gathering orb of light, and just as it bursts into a flash, Cara yanks me back.

I look back just in time to see four lights shooting off in random directions—but I barely notice, because right where the cairn stood is a glowing apparition of a wolf.

It's as big as a grizzly bear, and the ground begins to frost around its mighty paws. The beast bares its fangs and glares with glowing blue eyes.

"What is that?" I ask, fear making my voice tremble.

"Hungry. Now run!" Cara drags me away, and we both break into a sprint.

As we make our way back toward the house, the beast jumps through the air and lands in our path. She charges, jaws unhinged, and Cara instinctively tackles me and shields me with her body. The maw of the monster just barely misses her.

It turns on me and snarls.

I sprint away from Cara and the wolf gives chase. I make my way to the woods, reckoning that I can't outrun her, so my only chance is to try and confuse her by weaving through the trees, but she's fast, and continues to cut me off, forcing me back onto the main path.

Just as the wolf corners me once more, forcing my back up against a tree, something strikes her front left shoulder, causing her to fling her head back with a yelp.

I follow the monster's gaze to Cara, holding the wood recurve bow she had stowed in her case. Her quiver is strapped to her left hip, and she draws another arrow from it.

"Don't touch her!" Cara shouts as she fires, but this time the beast roars, and the arrow seems to be thrown off of its trajectory, landing broken off to the side.

As the wolf rushes her, I grab its tail with both hands.

She whips around and knocks me flat on my back. The monster stands over me, and I cover my face and cower, waiting for the blow that would inevitably come.

But nothing happens.

I peek from behind my hands just in time to see the nearby tree bend unnaturally and swing its branch out, batting the wolf away. As she recovers, several spears of ice, at least six feet long, rain down in a line to form a barrier around her.

I look toward the house, and the man from the house is standing there, arm outstretched, the tattoo on his hand glowing white.

The wolf howls and shatters the ice spears, baring her fangs toward the man. Before the last bits of ice can hit the ground, the man begins to walk forward, and with each step a bolt of lightning streaks from the sky toward the beast. She dodges each bolt, narrowly avoiding incineration, as rain begins to fall.

With a snarl, the wolf turns and runs off into the woods.

The man lowers his arm and his tattoo stops glowing. "Is anyone hurt?" he calls.

Cara rushes to my side and helps me to my feet as I reply, "We're okay!"

The man walks over to us. "What happened? What are you two doing here?"

"I was just . . . I thought it . . . I mean, my dreams," I stammer out. "Everything was identical except the cairn. I didn't *do* anything. I just put my hand on it and it collapsed!"

His face is strangely calm—curious, even, as he scrutinizes me. "What do you know about magic, kid?"

". . . Nothing," I say blankly. *Magic*? Is that really what this is?

He looks lost in thought, a shadow across his face as if he is recalling something painful. He reaches his hand out and holds it in front of me for a moment, studying me with his eyes.

"To break one of her spells by accident . . . yet you're not even a witch."

That pronoun catches my attention. "Her? The woman with the dark hair and that same tattoo? She pushed my hand onto the cairn and disappeared right before it broke."

The man's eyes bulge nearly out of his head and dart to my face. He looks away quickly and takes a couple of deep breaths, as if trying to compose himself. His evident anxiety is contagious, and I find myself getting nervous, too, wondering if I've done something bad by coming here.

"What are your names?" he asks eventually.

"I'm Selena."

"I'm Cara, I use she and her pronouns," Cara extends her hand, only for it to be promptly ignored.

"I am Seath Faolan, Consort to the late Witch of the Full Moon, Elatha Yukiko. I think we have some things to talk about, Miss Selena. Come by tomorrow afternoon with Miss Cara." He snaps his fingers, and a series of small, pale balls of light appear like stars along the path for illumination. "I will tell you all about that wolf you woke up and what to do if she comes back. And if you are willing to learn, I will teach you how to become a practitioner of magic. I will teach you how to become a witch."

III.

Consort

Waiting for school to end when you are intensely anticipating what comes after is agonizing. The subjects covered in class seem all the more dull, and the clock seems to tick away at half-speed. I can't help but fidget as the day bleeds by, waiting, waiting, *waiting*—waiting for school to end, mere hours from my whole world changing.

Perhaps I'm exaggerating a bit, but this feels monumental. Seath could make the trees bend at will, create lightning, make fairy lights—what else? He did mention that the cairn was some kind of spell. Would I learn how to do that? What even was it?

And the woman from my dreams—was that some kind of spell, too? Is that woman trying to talk to me? Elatha Yukiko. Her name rings like a bell through my head. Where is she now? How come Cara couldn't see her?

Seath called himself her consort. I pull out my phone and search the unfamiliar word. Google defines a consort as *'a wife, husband, or companion, in particular*

24

the spouse of a reigning monarch.' Does that mean he is her husband? Was she some kind of queen?

I have a thousand questions, and I'm eager to learn how to bend trees myself.

My phone buzzes, and I take it out to read under my desk in history class.

Cara writes, *'I can't sit still at all, I wanna go so badly'* followed by a medley of emojis.

'I know, I want to learn so badly!!1!' I type back.

'Be careful tho, we don't know this guy. Even if he can teach us magic, be safe.'

Cara and I are too excited by the time gym ends to even take the time to change afterwards—my purple track jacket and black shorts are fine for today's meeting, and Cara throws a white hoodie over her top and carries her bow case over her shoulder. Funnily enough, I have the same pink track pants as her at home somewhere, lost in my mess of a closet.

We walk to Seath's house only to find him waiting on the front porch with a steel grey button up shirt and crisp black slacks.

"Ladies," he calls. With a snap of his fingers, the front door of the house opens slowly.

He leads us inside. Cara and I stand in awe of the beautiful home. The interior is old fashioned, with weathered hardwood floors, navy wallpaper, and an ornate, silver chandelier in the foyer. The furniture is all dark wood, the upholstery all a pastel lavender or royal blue, and the walls are adorned with oil paintings. In my vision the details were fuzzy and difficult to discern, but being here, in the day, I can appreciate the haunting charm of the manor.

Seath leads us to the double doors left of the grand split staircase, leading to a sitting room with old fashioned couches arranged around an oak coffee table that sits upon a patterned rug. On the far wall is a mantle and fireplace, full of dry, unburnt logs.

He sits with the fireplace on his right, so we sit on the opposing couch facing him.

"I imagine you have questions," he says.

"I have so many I don't even know where to begin," I reply, staring at him. "But I guess if I had to pick one to start with it would be: is this real?"

His mouth twists into a wry smile. "That depends on your perspective, I suppose. Or more accurately, your imagination."

"What does that mean?" Cara asks, leaning forward.

"Magic is the art of applying will to imagination to influence the world. It is the power of creativity and ingenuity."

"So is magic real?" I press, my heart thumping.

Seath walks over to the mantle where a framed, faded photo rests. He pushes the frame to the ground, shattering the glass, but with a wave of his hand it is back on the mantle perfectly intact. He brings his hand up to the glass, and, somehow, removes the photo without disassembling the frame or even touching it at all.

He hands it to me—it's the woman from my dreams, except she is dressed normally in a pale blue summer dress with a straw hat. She's elegant and beautiful, but even like this she remains mysterious and mystical.

"Let's start with her," he says, dropping himself back into his seat. "Her name is Elatha Yukiko, and she was the Witch of the Full Moon. She died thirty years ago, but when she was alive, she was one of the most powerful witches around. My power comes from her."

"So you're married? That's what a consort is, right?" I ask.

"In magic, a witch is someone who can generate magic and create spells. And a consort is someone whom she has allowed unrestricted access to her powers. As consort to the Witch of the Full Moon, I can use the lingering dregs of her magic."

I turn every word of his over in my head, and I wonder what I should ask next. I suppose my most pressing question is; "Can I do magic?"

"What about me?" Cara asks.

"Well, you both can learn magic, but only one of you can become a witch," he explains, gesturing to me. "You must have a strong affinity to the moon if you were able to release the spell left behind by Yukiko, Miss Selena. Not to mention you seem to be having magical dreams—prophetic visions, potentially, ones we'll see about teaching you to interpret."

Then he adds, a bit softer, "Yukiko also had the ability to see the future, so that tells me you might be able to inherit her magical sigil."

The words fill me with elation. My mind races with possibilities, and I can't help but smile from ear to ear. "You're really going to teach me?"

"I will teach you magic on two conditions," he replies. "First of all, you let those spirits out, so if I teach you magic it will be your responsibility to collect them all."

"All?" Cara chimes in. "You mean the wolf? She only broke one cairn."

"And that cairn held five thrall spirits inside." At our confused faces, he explains, "Thralls are magical constructs that usually take the form of spectral animals, made by witches to serve different purposes. Yukiko used them to protect this manor, but in her absence they have gone rogue in their search for her. Each thrall will no doubt cause trouble throughout town until you can find and contain them."

I nod. "What's the other condition?"

"I am willing to train you every weekend provided you get written permission from your parents stating that they know where you are and what you are doing, and that they consent to this."

My heart sinks, and I recoil with a scowl. "What? Why!"

"Because if your parents aren't okay with this, then I'm the one who has to try to explain to the cops why I'm hiding little girls in my spooky house in the woods without parental permission or awareness, and I am not stupid enough to put myself in that position," he says. "That's how people end up arrested or on some kind of watch list."

"He's being fair, Selena," Cara says, putting her hand on my shoulder. "This rule is for our safety, too. Your parents will approve for sure!"

We agree with his terms, though I already know I won't tell my parents the truth.

As we leave, he gives us two sheets of paper with his name, address, and cell number for our parents. The whole walk home, even as I talk to Cara, I am thinking of what kind of lie to use.

I come home to find my mom and dad in the living room. Mom—fair-skinned with dark, straight hair like mine down to her waist—is sitting on the couch in an oversized hoodie and pajama pants, leaning forward and playing a video game on the big TV across from her, while dad reclines in the armchair on her left with a book in hand and a glass of red wine on the coffee table between them. Despite being well put-together socially, they sure do know how to relax at home.

"Mom, Dad, Cara and I wanted to join this sort of club, it's free, I just need a permission letter from you saying I can go."

Mom looks over at Dad out of the corner of her eye.

"What kind of club is it?" Dad asks, adjusting his glasses.

"An occult club," I lie. "It's going to be kind of like a history class, talking about stuff like witchcraft."

He studies my expression for a really long time, making nerves flutter to life in my stomach.

"I . . . I'm really interested in this stuff, you know, like fantasy stuff, and I thought it would be fun to learn more about it and . . . " I find myself searching for more things to say the longer he looks at me with his stern eyes. "Oh, it's also, you know, all about women, which is nice because a lot of my history classes only ever talk about men and . . . " My voice finally trails off.

His eyes dart to Mom then back to me. "When is it?" he asks skeptically.

"It's on Saturdays and Sundays." I watch them both, looking for any sign of what their answer will be.

Dad nods to Mom, who looks at me with her narrow black eyes and says, "Alright, we'll sign it. But keep us updated, yeah?"

IV.

Caveat

It's a chilly Saturday as I make my way to Seath's with an eager smile.

Cara opts for leggings and a tight verdant running jacket—she finds it easier to practice with her bow like that. I went in a different direction—skinny jeans and a baggy lavender hoodie.

Seath waits for us on the front steps like last time, wearing his leather coat over dark colors. He ushers us inside and leads us to the hallway under the grand staircase, to a set of double doors with the sigil of the full moon emblazoned on the wood. He stops at the door, letting out a deep sigh.

"What is it?" I ask, sensing his hesitancy.

"It's been thirty years since I've been in this room." He takes a decrepit key from the inside of his jacket and pushes it into the lock, and with a satisfying click, he heaves the stiff doors open.

It's the library from my dream—though it's much dustier, and the sigil on the floor by the great bay windows is faded. There is a small, round table and a large armchair facing the window, just on the other side of the sigil, and a wood-bound black book sits on the table.

To the left is another table, this one rectangular with six chairs scattered around it. Seath takes his jacket off and throws it over one of those chairs before walking over to the armchair and picking up the book from its side. He stares at the cover for a while, and though I can only see a sliver of his face from where I stand, it looks as if he is lost in bittersweet memory.

He places the book back down and turns to us as we sit at the big table facing him.

"Before you can practice magic, you have to understand a few things," Seath says, placing his hands flat on the table as he leans towards us. "There are two ways to use magic. The first way is through a magic circle. These circles were created by witches to be shared with other people, and each circle represents a specific spell, though how you use that spell is . . . shall we say, open to interpretation."

He raises his hand, showing the tattoo to us. "The second way is with one of these. This is a sigil. It represents the affinity and powers of a witch. With it, a witch can perform any type of spell without restriction as long as it falls under her affinity. It doesn't matter how strong or smart someone is. Magic is the power of imagination—of creativity and will. When it comes down to it, that is the only thing that matters. With it, you can do anything. Your power is limited only by your inhibitions."

"What do you mean, 'do anything?'" Cara asks.

Seath looks back at us with an intensity in his eyes to punctuate his words. "I mean anything." He walks over to the head of the table. "Now, there are some caveats to that."

"Caveats?" I ask.

"Well, limitations, so to speak. For starters, and this might seem obvious, but it is hugely important; you cannot do anything you don't believe you can do. If you believe something is impossible, then it will be."

He starts to pace slowly as he talks, his hands moving animatedly with every point. "You also have to understand that you are not the only magical thing around. The world itself is magical, and any attempt to influence or break nature or the laws of physics will be met with resistance. The more you try to break the world, the more resistance you face. That goes double if you try to perform spells that conflict with magic cast by other witches and magic users."

"Are there others?" I ask eagerly. "Other witches?"

It would be wonderful to meet other magical people and learn as much as I can from them. I feel like I've discovered a whole new world just hidden below the reality I've lived in up till now.

Seath, however, does not share my enthusiasm. The mention of other witches seems to send a dreadful shiver down his spine, and he seems to be unsure of how to answer.

"Well, naturally there are others," he says carefully, "but they are rare, and at least for now, it's unlikely you will meet them. There was a time when some witches could go their whole lives without meeting another magical practitioner. Some witches like to work together, others prefer to go it alone and stay away from their fellow magical beings. The Witch of the Full Moon was of the latter sort, and as such there are no other witches around these parts."

Something about his phrasing leaves me wondering if I'll find other witches in my time—or if they'll find me.

"You said breaking nature would be met with resistance; what do you mean?" Cara asks.

Seath seems relieved to move on from the topic. "In short, it's a test of will. If your willpower isn't strong enough to overcome nature, your magic will fail. There are some things that you just won't ever be able to do–"

"You said we could do anything," Cara interrupts.

"I said there are caveats. Theoretically, yes, you can do anything, but if you decided, for example, you wanted to destroy the world? You will fail no matter how hard you try. The innate magic of the earth would resist the attempt, and the planet has a stronger will than you do. Plus, there are ancient spells put in place thousands of years ago to protect from destructive magic like that.

"You also can't make someone stop existing or die instantly. The ancient spells, combined with the innate magic of the world, makes doing something like that extremely challenging. Even with a whole coven you would have a hard time making someone drop dead. Not that witches have, historically, had a difficult time murdering people when they felt like it, they just have to apply a little bit of creativity."

He stops and thinks for a minute, then speaks up again as if tacking on a note he had forgotten to mention.

"Oh, and you can't bring back the dead. Reanimating a dead body or even creating a new body is easy enough, but once a soul has left the corporeal world, you can't bring it back—not entirely anyways. Even with the most successful resurrections, something essential about that person, the thing that makes them . . . well, themselves, that part doesn't come back."

Cara nods meaningfully.

"So," I ask, excited to actually get started. "How do we actually *do* magic? Do I need, like, a big staff like Gandalf? Or do we need a wand?"

"He didn't use a wand," Cara notes, gesturing to Seath.

"Nothing like that. Any woman can become a spellcaster just by studying and learning to cast with magic circles and believing in the power. And when you become a witch, Miss Selena, you'll have this sigil, and with it, the possibilities will be limitless."

"Just women? What about you?" Cara asks, gesturing to his hand and the sigil upon it.

"Men cannot become witches or spellcasters. Men are incapable of generating or performing magic on their own, and can only use magic if they are granted power by a witch. They bear her sigil, and serve either as her consort—like myself—trusted with complete freedom with her powers, or as her vassal—granted a small, controlled fraction of her powers."

The word serve stands out most of all to me, it says a lot about how much he must revere Yukiko, even thirty years after her death.

"I think I've droned on long enough," he says with a clap. "It's time you try out a spell of your own."

36

"What are we going to learn? Will it be like DnD? Will we learn how to cast fireball? Oh, or are we going to learn how to make the tree attack stuff like you did?" I say, jumping from my chair.

Seath smirks, walking over to one of the bookshelves, retrieving a thick, green, leather-bound book with some plant artwork on the cover.

He drops the book on the table, throwing up dust. "You're going to learn how to take care of a houseplant."

V.

Frustration

Seath's instructions were simple. He asked us to open the green book to a particular page—a page which features Latin script on the left, and an elaborate circle with line art somewhat resembling a budding seed on the right—and meditate with the book as we plant and care for seeds he gave us.

He sits two mug-sized cups of dirt on the library table, and hands us each a single seed, explaining that mine is a blackberry, and Cara's is a red currant. We plant our seeds, water them, then sit back at the table, watching Seath expectantly.

He simply plucks up another book, though, and puts his feet up, reading without paying us any mind.

"Uh, Mr . . . I don't know what you want us to call you," Cara says. "What do we do now?"

He shrugs. "What do you think you should do?"

"What does this have to do with magic?" I press, getting a little agitated. This is *not* what I had in mind.

"I told you, keep the book open to that circle, focus on your plant, and just meditate with the book in mind. You can touch the circle if that helps you focus," he says, aloof as ever, seemingly bothered that I would have the audacity to even ask.

"Okay, but I don't understand how this helps us learn magic."

Without taking his eyes off of his book he just shakes his head. "I'm sure you'll get it eventually."

"But you said you'd teach us!" My hand slams on the table in frustration.

"I've taught you enough to get started. There is such a thing as over-explaining, you know." He looks at us over the top of his book. "Do whatever you think you need to do."

"Okay," Cara interrupts, turning to me. "Clearly he's not going to help us out, so let's just do what feels right."

She inspects the circle, running her fingers along the lines. The book seems to be in immaculate condition despite being left on its own with no care for thirty years. Perhaps there is some significance to that, though I'm not even really sure if books do require maintenance. On the other hand, old books always look brittle and yellow in movies, yet this one looks brand new.

"He said magic circles are like a mold for magic. Maybe if we focus hard enough on the circle, we can make the plants grow with magic?"

I nod. Seath did want us to 'take care of a houseplant', but he was and remains to be frustratingly vague on how he intends for us to do so. Focusing on using the circle to make the plant grow seems like a reasonable suggestion. Though despite that, even after hours of focusing, nothing happens. Around one o'clock, he sets his book down and stands, stretching and groaning dramatically.

"Alright, let's break for lunch. I'll order a pizza, is everyone good with pepperoni?"

"I'm vegan, I hope you understand," Cara says.

Seath rubs his brow with his fingers, pinching the bridge of his nose. "Of course you are."

"Sunshine Pizza does great vegan pizza, you should give it a chance! I bet you've never tried it," she teases.

I have to smile. Cara is always trying to win people over when it comes to doing something *right* or *moral*. She is rarely negative towards a person, but she tries to push them to try to be better—or her version of better, anyways. I often find myself agreeing with her, but I am just one of many people she's failed to convert to veganism. Still, I'll make the effort around her at least, even though I know she doesn't expect me to.

Seath is much less considerate. He grumbles and orders us food, ordering a 'real pizza' as he calls it for himself and getting us a vegan pie to split.

We wait for the food in the dining hall, which is back in the foyer, opposite of the sitting room we had found ourselves in on our last visit.

"I have a question," I say abruptly as we sit in the dining hall around the large table. "What happened to the wolf thrall?"

"I suppose he's off wandering the woods as we speak. You're eventually going to have to go and catch him, when you're ready." he replies. "Remember, it's your responsibility to fix that mess."

I feel a shiver of terror run down my spine as I recall the harrowing fight. "Why can't you do it?"

"I'm not the one who broke the spell, why should I fix it?" he says smugly. "Besides, it will be good training."

"But won't it be dangerous?" Cara chimes in, noticing my suppressed panic.

"I won't let you get hurt. But . . . I told you already; Yukiko, the Witch of the Full Moon, passed away. The magic she left behind for me is almost completely depleted. If this was ten years ago, that would be one thing, but now? After that last fight I don't have much in me. I could save you in a real pinch, but if I'm not careful, the last of Yukiko's magic will be depleted."

"If things were that dire maybe you shouldn't have wasted your magic creating those fairy lights for us, or making the doors open on their own!" I snap.

That got him flustered. His face screwed up as he snapped, "I did that so *you* would believe me when I told you magic was real."

"About the thralls," Cara interrupts, glancing between us. "Are they all wolves like the one we saw?"

Seath lets out a long exasperated sigh. "The cairn you so carelessly knocked over contained five animal spirits inside. There is the wolf, the owl, the skunk, the bat, and the raccoon. They were precious to Yukiko, and I will have to insist that you catch all of them."

I'm curious to know more—about Yukiko, the thralls, and everything else—but something tells me he doesn't want to talk about it. There's always an air of conflict about him when she comes up, a deep affection for her, and a deep sadness at her loss.

As the day goes on, the idea of facing that wolf and other beasts like her dominates my thoughts. Even after we eat, I am left to worry about how I could possibly capture five magical animals. It is consuming enough that I am completely unable to focus on my plant for the rest of the day, and even the next day when we return to the manor I cannot meditate.

Not only am I to somehow capture these monsters, but I feel like Seath isn't actually *teaching* us anything, and any time I try to ask him to explain more he brushes me off. By the end of the day on Sunday, my frustration has boiled into a burning rage inside me, making my whole body tense.

Seath gives us the green book to try and practice with on our own during the week, but I don't even want to look at it after staring at that stupid circle for a combined fourteen hours thus far. Still, I tuck it into my bag.

That night, I find myself unable to sleep, tossing and turning well past midnight. The fear and my anger fill my mind and leave me restless. Finally, at one in the morning, I drag myself out of bed and take the book with me out to the backyard, throwing on a bulky sweater against the chill. Our backyard is fairly plain— just a simple fenced in plot of patchy, yellowed grass with a little cedar patio. I sit at the patio table under the backyard light and open the book. I need to figure this thing out, or I feel like I'll lose it.

I look out at the grass and then back to the circle, trying to focus, but after five minutes of nothing happening my anger gets the better of me. "This is so stupid!" I spit out, slamming my fists against the open book.

As my hand makes contact with the magic circle, it lights up in a brilliant emerald green, and a wave of energy explodes from the book, knocking me out of my chair and shattering the bulb of the light above me. As I drag myself back to my feet, I notice the circle's glow fade to nothing, and I am left alone in the dark. I can feel my heart racing in my chest, and I'm scared to touch the book for fear of triggering another blast.

Taking a deep breath, I turn my phone's light on and reach out, picking the book up and inspecting it.

I've only barely looked at it before something catches my attention from the corner of my eye. I frown. Something seems off about the grass.

I shine my light out toward the yard, and all the yellowed patches are gone and the area is covered end-to-end in three-inch-high picture-perfect grass. I tread on it cautiously, yet in awe. The cool blades are crisp and healthy, tickling my feet as I walk across the yard. Crouching down, I inspect it, almost expecting it to be an illusion or feel fake, but it's all real.

I rise up, tears falling from my face. I can't even tell if I'm crying from joy or relief, but I don't care. As my giddiness and excitement starts to dissipate, I find myself feeling exhausted, and when I return to bed I'm asleep within seconds.

VI.

Kleptomaniac

I can barely keep my eyes open as I trudge along the path to school. I run into Cara at the school gates, just like always, and my exhaustion temporarily disappears as I rush to her.

"Hey—Wow, your eyes, were you up all night?" she says, perceptive as ever.

"I did it!" I blurt out, ignoring her question. "I was trying to practice with the circle last night and out of nowhere there was this, like, burst of light and I fell out of my chair and I accidentally made my entire backyard turn into the most perfect lawn ever!"

"Really?" she asks in awe. "How?"

"No idea! I tried to replicate it this morning, but nothing happened."

As we walk into the school, I notice all the students talking and forming little crowds, or running off down the halls. There is a deafening sea of agitated voices that blend together too well to interpret.

"What's happening?" I ask.

Cara looks around, perplexed. "I don't know."

As we turn the corner of the entryway, the source of the commotion starts to become apparent. Every single locker has been broken open, their contents strewn about. Cara and I look at each other. Without a word, we rush to her locker on the second floor. Just like all the others it's broken with the lock ripped off. Her books and papers are scattered, and she kneels down in the mess to look through them.

"Gone, they're all gone!" she panics.

"What's gone?"

"All my photos and the drawings you gave me, the ones from last summer? I put them up in my locker and they're gone!"

"Who would steal pictures?" I ask.

Suddenly, I feel a strange, cold tension on the back of my neck, and I spin around on my heels. Nothing out of the ordinary is visible, and yet I can feel that there is something there. I try to focus, and I feel a strange tingling in my chest as my eyes lock in one direction, but the feeling quickly fades.

Snapping out of my trance, I kneel down and help Cara collect her things and store them back in her locker. We head to my locker next, though I keep very little in it. I can't help but notice that I am also missing something—a novel that was gifted to me by Cara on my last birthday.

The bell rings, and we head off to our first period class together. Most of the student body ignores the bell at first, until the stern voice of the principal sounds over the speakers ordering us all to disperse.

I find my seat by the window, while Cara sits in her assigned seat in the front row. The teacher, a tall lady in a pencil skirt with rigid posture and her black hair in a tight bun, leans against her desk to address us.

"So, by now you've seen the state of our halls. The school was found like this this morning, and it seems someone broke in and vandalized all the lockers. Right now, we don't know anything about who did it or why, or what's missing. Before you leave today, please visit the office and give the secretary a list of all your missing items, along with their estimated monetary value. The list will be given over to the police. As for your locks, I will be providing you all with new ones tomorrow morning. For the foreseeable future, please don't store anything valuable in your lockers."

I take my phone out under my desk and text Cara *'What do you think happened?'*

'I don't know, this is crazy. Maybe it was some drunk adults?' she replies.

'I felt something weird before, and I have this weird urge that I should come back here tonight.'

'Do you think it could be something magical?'

'I don't know. Maybe.'

I feel the same compulsion that led me to Seath, the same feeling that guides my steps in my dreams. It's this inner sense that something is here and calling out to me, and I am drawn toward it instinctively.

The feeling haunts me all day, keeping me from focusing in class. After school, Cara and I walk to the gates and take a look back.

"What do you think?" she asks.

I can feel something . . . vague in the school. Whenever I look at the building, it's like a shiver shoots up my spine. I feel that same compulsion from before urging me to return at night, but I also feel a sense of anxiety around the unknown.

"Let's come back after dark. It could be the wolf. They were made by the Witch of the Full Moon, so maybe they can only be active at night?"

"That makes sense," Cara replies. "How about 9 o'clock?"

"See you then!"

One thing about Cara I've always found amusing is the logic she operates on. She is someone who believes in dressing for the occasion—and for the occasion of breaking into the school at night, she comes prepared, wearing tight pants, a hoodie, a beanie, running shoes, and gloves, all in black. Her quiver is strapped to her hip, and I can tell how nervous she is by how tightly she grips her bow.

I brought my backpack, though the only things in it are the magic book and a pry bar from my dad's toolshed.

"So, how do we get in?" she asks.

I take out the pry bar. "Let's break in around the back."

As we walk around the school using our phones for light, I feel my skin crawl. I get the sense that something is watching me, but I can't see anything around. The unnerving feeling appears contagious, as Cara's hands are visibly shaking, too.

As we approach the back doors I get a sharp shiver that runs down my spine—a feeling that screams at me to run.

"Cara, something doesn't feel right," I say, hesitating as I stare at the back door.

She turns to face me. "Wha–"

The shiver returns, even more potent than before, and on sheer instinct I leap forward and tackle Cara to the ground. At that very moment something comes crashing through the doors, tearing them from their hinges. The broken metal and glass sails harmlessly over our bodies, and when we look out toward the field, we can see an ethereal ghostly blob.

The creature un-balls itself, and I can see that it is not formless, but cherubic. It turns to look at us, and I find myself staring, mouth agape, at a giant spectral raccoon. She arches her back and stares at me.

Cara and I pull each other to our feet. The raccoon inches forward.

"She's staring at me," I blurt out.

The wolf chased me, too, now that I think about it. I look around. The monster is four feet tall on all fours, and evidently very strong. If I stay close to Cara, then she'll be in danger, too. Now is no time to be afraid.

I broke the spell—Cara cannot get hurt because of me.

"Get ready to shoot her!" I say as I throw my pry bar at the monster as I sprint away from it. I run parallel to the building, and she lunges and swipes with her six-inch claws, leaving deep cuts in the brickwork.

I know I have no hope of outrunning her. But it occurs to me that every time the raccoon has attacked thus far she has lunged, so she may struggle to make sharp turns.

I throw myself to the left, praying my theory is correct, and I just narrowly avoid being swiped by her claws.

At that moment, an arrow flies over, hitting the monster in her left arm. She hisses and stares down Cara, who fires again. This time the raccoon slaps the arrow out of the air. I roll away and pull my bag from my back to retrieve the book.

The raccoon flexes, shattering the arrow in her arm, then she charges Cara, unphased by a third arrow striking her chest.

I open the book to the magic circle and place my palm against it, but nothing happens. Cara dodges a swipe, but her bow is knocked from her hands.

I try to focus, to make anything happen, but the circle won't respond to my wishes.

The monster shoulder-checks Cara, knocking her down, and stalks over her with her claws raised.

"Do something!" I shout at the book as my heart thumps so loudly in my chest that all other noise is drowned out.

The circle glows, and the grass under the raccoon grows dramatically, tangling around her three grounded paws. The monster immediately snaps her attention to me and runs at me full tilt. I try to use the book again, and the circle glows, causing the grass to grow rapidly, but not nearly thick or tall enough to trip or slow the beast. The racoon slaps the book out of my hands, then backhands me in the stomach, sending me tumbling across the ground.

I cough and feel incredibly nauseated from the impact. I gasp for air and suck in as much as I can. When I look up, I notice the raccoon clutching the book in her left paw. She chitters and hisses at us, then runs away back inside the school.

Cara retrieves her bow then runs over to help me up. "Are you hurt?"

"No," I say breathlessly. "But that thing stole Seath's book. Are you okay? I'm sorry I couldn't do more to help you."

She hugs me tightly for a moment. "You saved me. And you actually used a real spell, didn't you?"

"Yeah, but the book's gone now."

"I think it's time we tell Seath about this," she says. "Let's get out of here."

VII.
Branding

Seath stares at us blankly. It seems like he can't decide between bewilderment, anger, or pity. He settles on some amalgamation of the three, shaking his head at us and pacing in the sitting room of his home.

"So let me get this straight—after successfully performing a single spell, you two thought you could take on one of the thralls with a bow and *grass*?" The anger seems to win, then, and he shouts, "That spell is for manipulating the growth of plants and shrubs! It is not intended to be used for combat."

"We also lost the book," I mumble under my breath.

"Oh, spectacular!" Seath tenses up and he firmly grasps the back of the couch in front of us, and for a moment it looks as though he's fighting the urge to fling it. "On top of everything else, you lost a one-of-a-kind, 1200 year old book written by the Grandmother of Potioneering, the former Witch of the Woods, Lady Elixir herself, Wulfflæd."

"We're sorry," Cara says, her hands in her lap and head bowed.

"It's my fault," I say. "I didn't know what we were up against. I didn't know that what I felt was a thrall."

He lets out a loud, breathy sigh. "This is partially my fault. Your magical senses are pretty sharp. You might be new, but you've been touched by magic somehow, considering your prophetic dreams of Yukiko. I should have realized you would be more sensitive to magic than most."

"What can we do?" Cara asks, finally raising her chin.

"For now, leave it."

"We can't," I say. "That thrall is terrorizing the school! We have to do something."

"Can't you at least scare her off, like the wolf?" Cara adds, looking up at him pleadingly.

He shakes his head. "Chances are you scared her, anyway. She's taken everything she sensed value in, so she's probably hiding somewhere protecting her loot. She won't actively cause trouble, at least for now."

I rise to my feet in a huff. "When will we be able to do something about this? If we leave her alone, someone else could get hurt!"

"She won't attack anyone else, though she might steal a lot more stuff, mischievous little furball that she is." A half-grin spread across Seath's mouth. "She only responded to you because she sensed the powers of the moon inside you, but you need to learn a lot more before you're ready. You'll need a grimoire, to start; a spellbook with magic circles for spells outside of the jurisdiction of your sigil. You'll need to adopt your sigil, too, of course, and finally you will need to find a familiar. Cara will also need to have a grimoire. As good as she is with a bow, non-magical weapons can only harm thralls, not defeat them."

"Did Yukiko have a grimoire?" Cara asks.

Seath nods and holds his hand open, causing a black book to appear. I recognize it from the library—it sat on the table beside the armchair in front of the bay window. Just by looking at it, I can tell it is a very old book.

Upon further study, it features a title in what looks like Japanese, along with an illustration of an owl surrounded by a circular representation of the eight phases of the moon. On the back is the sigil of the full moon, along with the image of a wolf. All the line art and lettering is silver. The book has a clasp built into the covers to hold it closed.

"So why can't we just use that one?" Cara asks. "At the very least Selena could use it, since she's supposed to inherit Yukiko's powers, right?"

Seath did say something like that before, though not exactly. He said I could inherit her sigil, and I'm not entirely sure what that means.

"A grimoire is unique to each practitioner. You have to build it yourself, in order to grow your magical abilities. You wouldn't be able to understand what most of these spells are capable of. But more than that, there's a reason I didn't show you how to use the spell from Wulfflæd's research journal. If I did, then when you tried the spell yourselves you would have just copied me. Magic is about imagination, remember? You can't become powerful by just copying what others have done. Besides, here." He tosses the book to me. "Try to open it."

The clasp won't open, and no amount of force will budge it. "I can't!"

"Her grimoire is sealed with powerful magic—no one alive has the power to open it, not even me. To my knowledge, only one person besides Yukiko has the ability to bypass it, and she's gone now, too."

I hand the book back to Seath. I want to ask who this other person was, but seeing Seath's lingering, pained expression as he turns it over in his hands, it feels best to leave it alone for now.

"Come with me, I have something to show you," Seath says.

Cara and I follow Seath back to the library room. He returns Yukiko's grimoire to its original place and picks up something from the long table that he quickly hides behind his back. As he approaches us, he holds out two beautiful books—one black and one a dark, reddish brown.

"They are bound in vegan leather because I know you'd be upset otherwise," he says, handing me the black book. "Which costs more and is way less natural than real leather, by the way."

The cover is soft and flexible, with a long strap to hold it closed when not in use. I flip through the virgin pages, releasing the distinctive earthy smell of new books.

Cara smiles. "Thank you. I know you don't really share my beliefs, so I appreciate you going out of your way."

Her genuinity seems to take Seath aback, and he can only look away from her and mutter, "It was nothing."

We sit at the big table following his gesturing, and he places a white book with elaborate sketch artistry on the cover down between us, opening it to an early page.

"This is a neat little spell, and it's going to go on page one of both of your grimoires."

The circle depicts a gritty feather and an inkwell inside of an array with a triangle—each corner leading to a rune along the path of a thin circle, with the whole image surrounded by a thicker one. The thick outer circle is incomplete, with the line drawn fading slowly to nothing as it travels clockwise.

"What does it do?" Cara asks. "It looks interesting."

"It was created by an old draftswoman to help the other witches in her coven who were less artistically gifted," Seath says. "In short, it's an ink spell. You can use it to copy any text or image from one book to another. Use it to copy the magic circle into your grimoires."

Cara and I both touch the magic circle with our hands. For a while, nothing happens. Then the circle lights up, and in a flash an exact copy is formed in Cara's book. She squeals in amazement as she inspects it with her hands, checking the underside of the page.

A tinge of jealousy creeps in my mind as I force a celebratory smile for her sake. She did it so fast—does that mean I'm doing something wrong?

I keep trying, focusing on the circle and concentrating, imagining it appearing in my book, too, but nothing happens.

Seath drags a chair right next to me and sits close enough that our shoulders are touching. "Imagine your magic is like a big cloud of formless energy, and you can make the cloud go anywhere you want."

"Okay," I say, the beginnings of a cloud forming in my mind.

"You are treating the magic circle as a window, you're looking through it and wondering why it's not doing anything with your cloud," he continues. "But the circle is not a window. It is a door. Open the door, and push your cloud of magic through it."

I close my eyes for a second and imagine an aura of swirling colors, almost like an aurora borealis, radiating from my body. I imagine directing it in different ways, stretching it out and retracting it, until I am comfortable that this mass of light is completely in my control. I open my eyes and watch the circle. I try pushing my imaginary aura toward it, but nothing happens.

"Don't look at the book. Don't look at the circle. Feel it."

I close my eyes again and reconstruct the image of the magic circle in my mind, and practice pushing my aura through its center.

I open my eyes once more and take a deep breath. I can feel it—the invisible aura that I'd imagined. I push it toward the circle, but nothing happens again. My eyebrows pull together. I try to focus my eyes on just the circle until the book becomes fuzzy and out of focus. The strain hurts my head, but I'm determined to push through. I know I can this, I can feel it.

I focus on the blank point at the tip of the feather within the circle, until the circle itself becomes fuzzy, too. I push my energy through that spot, and it takes shape. I snap out of my trance, and the magic circle in the white book is glowing. As I look at my own book, the circle is recreated on the blank page, a perfect copy.

I jump from my chair and shriek, "I did it!"

"Did you ever struggle with the botanical spell?" Seath asks.

"I did. I couldn't pull it off until the last second."

"Magic can escape your control when you're very emotional. That can make certain spells much easier to perform, but being able to control when you do magic is infinitely better. Once you have your sigil, control will be very important. Without it, you'll do more harm than good."

With this new spell in hand, we copy several other magic circles from different books, including a spell that could detect the presence of magic around us, a spell for creating fire, a spell for purifying water, a magic circle designed to create a familiar, and finally a minor healing spell. That one featured two colliding swirls, surrounded by a decagon and then a circle, and a series of lines forming a geometric array of triangles in the background.

Cara and I close our books and I lean back in my chair, exhausted. Each use of the drawing spell makes my body feel tired and drained, as if I had just gone through gym class a dozen times.

"Tired?" Seath says smugly. We nod in unison in reply. "Magic will do that to you. Utilizing your powers will drain your stamina, so especially when you're new to all

58

this you need to be mindful that you don't push yourselves too hard."

That makes sense. I always felt like I didn't sleep well enough after having one of my dreams about Yukiko, and those dreams are magic. I was also tired after I first made the botany spell work, too.

"Alright, you've done well and I think now you can finally brand yourself with your sigil," Seath says, placing his hand on my shoulder.

"What does that mean?" I ask. Cara watches intently.

"It means you'll get one of these," he says, gesturing to the sigil on the back of his hand. "Once you have it, you'll be able to do magic related to the moon without a circle."

"Will I have a tattoo, too, then? Like that one?" I ask hesitantly.

"To use the sigil it has to be branded on your body."

"Why can't I just put it in my grimoire and use it that way?"

"You just can't," Seath says dismissively. "It doesn't work that way, the sigil has to be more directly connected to your spirit and your mind. It has to be a part of you."

"I–I can't," I stammer. "If I came home with a tattoo my parents would kill me."

"You're just going to have to explain to them that it's a part of your studying of magic," Seath says. When I still hesitate, he presses, "This is an essential step, there cannot be any half measures here. If you need, you can take tonight to talk to them about it so they aren't surprised."

I stand up with my book, my hands shaking as I step back from the table. "I just can't do it, okay?"

Seath narrows his eyes. He walks over to the shelves and retrieves a small leather bound book, opening it to a page near the middle.

"Are you hiding something from me?" he asks, invoking a spell from the book.

I blurt out– "Yes I am." –without even thinking, as if the words are forced from my lips.

"What is it that you do not want me to know?"

I can feel the book activating once more. It feels like pressure inside my skull—as if some invisible force is squeezing the truth out of my brain.

I can't stop myself, I hurl out the words, "I lied to you about telling my parents. I told them this is a school club about history, they don't know I've been talking to you or learning magic."

Once I finish, I feel weak in the knees and woozy, and a primal fear grows in my chest.

"What did you do to her?" Cara demands, rushing over to me.

"It's a truth spell. It compels the person to respond to any question the caster asks honestly," he says, something hard entering his voice. He turns to me. "You lied to me."

"How could you–" I start.

"No! This is where you listen!"

He scowls as he steps toward us. "I agreed to share my knowledge of magic under some very simple conditions—conditions I laid out for my safety and peace of mind, as well as yours. You betrayed my trust and you didn't respect my boundaries. Our lessons are over. I want both of you out of my house, and I don't want to see either of you again until you're ready to do things properly."

I pull myself from Cara and storm off, throwing the door open on my way. I keep my back to both of them so they can't see the tears forming in my eyes.

Without direction from Seath, I'm not exactly sure how to go about developing my grimoire. It occurs to me that having magical power by itself isn't enough; having a teacher makes a whole world of difference. As I lay in bed and browse aimlessly on my phone, I wonder how I could even find someone else who does magic.

VIII.
Celly

It's been almost a week, yet moping in school and at home has produced no good ideas. Seath mentioned other witches, but he stressed there were none nearby. It's not like I could just Google *magic teachers in your area!* and find someone new to guide us.

I look over at Cara, who sits at my desk with her grimoire open in her lap and my drawing tablet on the desk before her. She pairs it to the computer, so that the screen mirrors what the tablet sees.

"What are you doing?" I ask.

"Well, this spell inscribes whatever we want to copy onto a blank page right? I wonder how that would work with a computer. I wonder how technology and magic mix together. Could it mix together?" She stares intently at her book.

She makes an interesting point, though I'm quick to point out, "You didn't answer my question."

"Oh, I'm going to use this spell on your drawing tablet to see if it recreates the image in Kreate."

"What if that breaks the tablet?"

Cara hesitates. "I didn't think of that, I'm sorry."

I think for a moment, then shrug. "You know what? I'm curious. Do it."

Cara focuses for a minute, and I watch the blank canvas on the screen of my computer. Suddenly, the Kreate app starts to glitch out and recreate a pixel-perfect rendition of the drawing spell.

"That's amazing!" I say. "So it works?"

"Seath did say magic works off of imagination. So, instead of imagining the spell imprinting on your tablet, I imagined the spell using your tablet to recreate the image in the app's canvas."

I grin. "It's kind of funny, the original creator of the spell probably had no idea how we'd be using it today."

"To be fair, I don't think the inventor of the computer ever imagined us drawing magic circles on it either," she replies with a smirk.

"Now for the real question—can you invoke the spell through the computer?" I ask, hopping up from my bed.

I walk over and grab one of my school notebooks, opening it up to a point where the left page has notes and the right is blank. I focus on the book and touch the screen. I do what Seath taught me and push my magical energy through the circle, imprinting the resulting form onto the blank page. Sure enough, the computer screen grows brighter for a moment, then the notes from the left page are copied perfectly on the right.

"Huh, I wonder what other spells can work with our devices?" I muse.

Cara leans back in her chair. "You know, you could maybe even turn your phone into a grimoire like this. It would be more compact than a traditional journal. Plus, you have your phone assistant to help you find stuff."

I laugh a little, setting the notebook down and flipping through my grimoire next. "I think my phone might need an intelligence upgrade before that can happen."

Suddenly, my grimoire lights up and flies from my hand, and I stumble backward, dropping my phone. The device lifts from the ground and levitates above me, and the screen distorts and scrambles.

Strange electronic noises fill the air, a buzzing that makes static crawl across my skin.

"What's happening?" Cara asks, shooting to her feet.

"I don't know!" I say, crawling back from the device.

The screen warps into a pixelated, blank white silhouette. The faceless animation seems to move its hands around and study itself for a moment.

"Wha–" I breathe out, but the device interrupts me.

"Hello Selena, my name is S-111308A. How may I be of service?" the device asks in a generic robotic woman's voice.

"What just happened?" I ask, bewildered.

"I cannot seem to find an answer in my database, would you like me to search the internet?"

"Uhh, Selena?" Cara says, picking up my grimoire. "I think I know what happened."

She holds it open to a particular page. The spell has six rings containing geometric art representing the sun, the moon, the stars, the heart, the mind, and the sea, all arranged along the points of a hexagon. A design like the Vitruvian Man forms the centerpiece. Surrounding everything is a ring with four smaller circles, each with geometric representations of the cardinal directions.

The spell for creating familiar spirits.

"You're a . . . You're my familiar?"

"That is correct," the phone replies.

"Did I create you?"

"I was manufactured in a plant in Vietnam."

"I don't think you can technically create a familiar, they have to already exist," Cara says, kneeling down beside me. "I think you're just forming a magic bond and elevating the mind of an already-living animal that you're close to."

"But this isn't an animal," I say, gesturing to the phone. "And it's not alive!"

"Well, it's kind of alive," Cara retorts. "I mean, depending on how you define life. It's not organic, but who says something has to be organic to be alive?"

I might be more interested in discussing Cara's theories on consciousness, if not for the living cell phone floating in the middle of my room.

"What do we call you?" I ask the phone.

"My name is S-111308A, according to my records."

Cara gives me a sassy smile. "Isn't that just the default device name? You didn't bother to rename your phone?"

Ignoring Cara, I ask, "Is it too late to rename you?"

"What would you like my new name to be?"

I look at Cara, who shrugs. "It's your decision."

Surely I can just assign a placeholder name for now? I don't know how any of this works and I'm still mentally going over the fact that I brought my cell phone to life.

"I guess I can call you . . . Celly?"

"Acknowledged, my name is Celly."

"Celly, why do you look like a blank avatar?" Cara asks.

"I have no data on what I should look like."

"I guess that makes sense," I say, pulling myself up and helping Cara stand. I sit at my desk and start typing on the computer. "You know, you give me pixie vibes. If I show you a drawing, Celly, can you make yourself look like that?"

Cara chimes in, asking, "Can you even see, Celly?"

"I can see through both my front and rear facing cameras, so I will do my best to make my avatar resemble whatever it is you show me," the device says.

I pull up a saved drawing of mine featuring a techno-punk fairy with short lavender hair and robotic pixie wings. Celly's avatar slowly warps to resemble a pixelated version of the drawing.

"What are your gender pronouns, Celly?" I ask.

66

"I do not have a gender, Selena."

I suppose I walked right into that one. Still, I don't quite feel comfortable referring to Celly as an inanimate object anymore, so using 'it' doesn't seem quite right.

"Do you have any preference for pronouns or gender?"

"None whatsoever."

Cara puts her hand on my shoulder. "How about we just use they/them pronouns then, if that's alright with you? I don't think either of us want to use any dehumanizing language with you now that we know you're sentient."

"Acknowledged!" The avatar seems to smile at us.

IX.
Nightstalker

I can feel the uncomfortable sense that someone is watching me as I slowly come out of sleep. As I open my eyes, I am treated to my phone levitating by my face, with the avatar's big eyes staring at me.

I let out a startled yelp and recoil before I remember the events of the previous night.

"Did I startle you, Selena?" Celly asks.

I sigh and rub my face. "It's okay, I just forgot you were alive for a second."

I hear a groan coming from the mess of pillows and blankets on my right. I look over and see Cara sprawled out beside me.

"Is Cara okay?" Celly asks, floating over to her. She groggily swats at them until they fly back over to my side.

"She's not a morning person," I whisper, stifling a laugh. "So, how does this work with you, Celly? Do I, like, need a new phone now or something, or, like, what do I do when I need to use you like normal?"

Celly points to my recents button. "If you tap there and close the app, you will put me in sleep mode. From there, you may continue to use all of my usual functions as normal. If you wish to wake up my sentient form as you see it now, you simply have to tap the Celly app I made for you. As long as the app is active, either in the background or the foreground, I will be awake and available to you, so you can access all of your data and apps while talking to me if you wish."

"That's very convenient."

For the time being I put Celly to sleep and get out of bed, being careful to step over Cara who has already drifted back to sleep. As she naps her morning away, I shower, dress warm, and meet my mom in the kitchen.

She has her hair down and wears a cute fuzzy white sweater over black leggings. As I walk into the kitchen, I see her leaning against the far counter with a big mug full of peppermint tea.

"Hey Snowflake, is Cara still sleeping?" she asks with a warm smile.

"Of course," I say with a nod. "She hates waking up in the morning."

"It's Saturday, don't you girls have your thing today?" she says, taking a sip.

Seath is probably still mad at us, but I can't tell her that. Thinking on the fly, I come up with, "Mr. Faolan said he's sick."

"That's a shame. When he's feeling better, maybe I should stop by and see him."

That sets my alarm bells off. "What? Why?" I squawk out awkwardly.

Mom shrugs. "Well, this is the first teacher who's gotten you to care about an extracurricular. He must be pretty special, right?"

"That's not true!" I say, perhaps a little too aggressively. "What about book club?"

Mom scoffs. "You only go because Cara goes. This thing with Mr. Faolan is something you've been passionate about. I've never seen you so motivated."

"I guess."

"So," she says, leaning over on the kitchen island with a sly grin, "is there any reason I can't meet him? Are you afraid I'll embarrass you?"

"I never said you couldn't, I just think it's weird, that's all."

She drops the subject and makes me a cup of tea as well, and we sip them together in silence as I wait for Cara to wake up. Eventually, we hear the heavy creaking of footsteps, but Mom can tell by the sound that it's Dad, and she leaves me alone to go and see him. Dad always sleeps in on Saturdays—according to Mom, it's the one day of the week he doesn't need to set an alarm, and she always encourages him to sleep a little later than usual.

After what feels like hours, Cara finds the strength to wake up. It takes her a while to shower and drag herself down to the kitchen, so in anticipation, I make her a cup of coffee the way I know she likes—no dairy, three sugar.

She walks in and mutters a "thank you" as she grabs it and walks through to the living room, sitting on the couch cross-legged and looking utterly miserable. I sit beside her, turned on the couch to face her, waiting for her to get far enough into her drink to return to her normal bubbly self.

"So, tonight's the night?" she asks. "Are you sure about doing this without Seath? Maybe we should reach out to him." She pauses, then adds, "What if we get hurt?"

"He kicked us out of his house, he's done with us," I spit out. I'm still bitter at how he reacted. He doesn't understand, and it's not fair to take away my magical training over something so stupid.

"Come on, you know that's not true," she says. "I'm sure if you just tried talking to him, you two could work this out. In fairness, we did violate a very reasonable boundary of his."

Cara's a good friend. I know that what she really means is *I* violated his boundary, but I know she's only saying 'we' so that I don't feel like she's blaming me. It's a shame I understand her so well, otherwise that would have probably worked.

"I don't want to talk about him," I say with a shake of my head. "Let's just focus. Tonight, we will go after the raccoon thrall and get that book back. We're a lot more prepared this time. We can use the fire spell, plus Celly will help us."

"I won't lie, I think it's a mistake not to tell Seath," Cara says. "But if you're set on going, I want to make sure you're safe."

That night, as we stalk around the back of the school in our dark clothes and I hold the pry bar tightly in my hands, I am hit with a sense of deja-vu. As we approach the previously smashed doors, we find they are still not replaced, and instead the entrance is blocked by a blue sheet taped over the doorframe. That eerie feeling from before returns. She's definitely inside.

First, I activate Celly's app, allowing them to levitate overhead.

"Celly, please turn your flashlight on and help us see in the dark," I say, and the light immediately flicks on.

Then I nod to Cara, who opens her grimoire and holds her left hand out. The sheet starts to burn up and melt, until a gap big enough for us to walk through is left and the edges are singed.

We walk into the dark halls of the school, and I flip my grimoire open to a circle that looks like two painted lines swirling from the outer circle to form the shape of an eye, with a hexagonal iris. When I activate the spell, I can suddenly detect exactly where the raccoon thrall is. "Second floor!"

Cara takes her bow out and gets her quiver ready, then we speed walk toward the stairs. We reach the cafeteria doors on the second floor, then hesitate for a moment, sensing the presence of magic beyond, but I look to Cara who nods back at me, and that's all the courage I need to throw the door open.

The cafeteria is still and empty. The chairs are all neatly stacked on top of the tables, and it's cleaner than I've ever seen during the day.

"She's in here," I say with a frown. "I can feel it."

"I see no signs of activity here," Celly says.

Cara's eyes narrow as she cautiously walks across the room. "This one has a habit of surprising us."

As I reach the center of the room, I hear a sickening creak from above, and I stop dead in my tracks. I look up and see the ceiling tiles warping. "You're not serious . . ."

The tiles begin to buckle and the light fixtures start cracking and popping. I jump away just as it all collapses above, under the oppressive weight of the bestial raccoon. She lands with an earth-shaking thud, debris raining down harmlessly on and around me as I fall to my knees.

I scurry back to my feet, and find myself mere inches from the snarling monster.

Cara wastes no time firing an arrow, but the beast anticipates it and slaps it from the air, then launches a nearby table at her.

"You won't beat us this time!" I open my book to reveal a flame spell. Holding the book open I raise my hand, and a bolt of fire shoots out and hits the thrall, spreading and igniting down her entire left side.

The raccoon whips around to face me and charges, still aflame, and I send another bolt of fire directly into her face, but she shrugs it off.

"She will not stop Selena, get out of the way," Celly warns.

I dive left to avoid her.

This time, however, the thrall is better prepared—her body turns to the side, and as she slides across the floor. A massive paw reaches out and grabs my left shin, and I can feel a searing pain rip through my whole body, starting from there. The creature swings and releases me, and I go crashing through another table and slide into the wall.

Everything is a blur. I can't seem to focus at all. My head is pounding, and my leg burns. I can't breathe for what feels like forever, and despite knowing Celly is calling out to me I can't hear their voice.

I try to raise my head but I am immediately nauseated. Finally, I gasp and allow air to rush into my lungs, but it feels like sandpaper and makes me cough violently.

"Selena!" Celly calls, their robotic voice cracking from its usual monotone cadence. "What should I do? You are injured."

I try to stand, but when I put weight on my left leg it feels like pure agony and I collapse. Instead, I sit up, pulling myself against the wall. Looking down, I realize that the raccoon's claws cut into my skin and I'm bleeding. The sight makes me even more sick and dizzy.

I look up and see the monster holding Cara up by her wrists. She looks battered and weak. For a moment I fear that the thrall may hurt her further, but instead something catches her attention. The beast drops Cara and runs away.

"Cara!" I croak out. "Cara, can you hear me?"

At that moment, a familiar voice fills the air. "She's going to be okay, but first we have to stop you from bleeding."

Seath walks into the cafeteria, using magic fairy lights to illuminate the space. He kneels beside me and holds out his hand, and the pain in my leg intensifies so much that I scream, gripping his shoulder as hard as I possibly can.

Despite the pain, the cuts in my leg rapidly scab over and fade, and I can feel my dizziness going away. As Seath lowers his hand, the pain dissipates to an aggressive throbbing, and he walks over to Cara.

I use the wall as a crutch to help me stand. It hurts to walk, but I can put pressure on my leg without collapsing.

I limp over to Cara, who is sitting up after just coming out of a daze.

"Is she okay?" I say as tears stream down my face.

Seath nods. "Of course she is. She's one tough girl."

"Sorry," Cara says weakly, rubbing her head. "She caught me off guard."

"I'm sorry!" I cry out, dropping beside her to hug her tightly.

Celly flies over, observing. "I am sorry I couldn't help, Selena."

"It's okay, Celly" I say through my tears. I turn to Seath. "How did you find us?"

Seath remains silent for a moment, staring mouth agape at Celly, then he furrows his brow and lets out a heavy, world-weary sigh. "A cellphone? Really?"

"Seath! How did know we were here?" I press.

"Cara texted me what you were up to," Seath says. "She didn't want you to know, but I thought saving your life trumped breaching her confidence."

"It did, thank you," she replies.

Seath lets out a heavy sigh. "Alright, both of you, let's get out of here before we all get arrested. We can talk about how unbelievably stupid this plan of yours was tomorrow, at the estate. Don't make me come looking for you," he says, picking me up and carrying me out as Cara and Celly trail behind.

X.

Trust

As Cara and I walk side by side on this brisque morning, I wonder if the scars on my shin will be permanent. Though my wounds are more or less healed, my leg still hurts even the following day. It hurts to walk, and I have a difficult time hiding my limp from my parents. Cara is bruised all over, but is overall alright. Seath explained the previous night that the healing spell can only accelerate the natural healing process, and it can't eliminate pain.

Seath is waiting to talk to us. He didn't say much after he carried me home the previous night, just that he wanted to see us today. I couldn't tell if he is angry, disappointed, both, or neither. I'm not sure what to say to him today. What can I say? What *should* I say?

Cara looks stressed, too. I've never seen her look so serious. Perhaps she's also working through what she wants to say.

"Cara, can we talk about Seath?" I say finally, fidgeting with my fingers.

"What is it?" she asks, not looking at me.

"Why didn't you tell me you texted him?"

She hesitates for a moment. "I didn't think you would understand why."

My brow furrows as I snap out, "How am I supposed to understand if you won't talk to me about it?"

She stops, turning on her heels to face me. "I did try to talk to you! I said we should talk to Seath, and you refused to try and apologize to Seath. You were wrong and you didn't want to admit it!"

I can see her eyes welling up with tears and her bottom lip quivering. I take a step back. I feel like her outburst has robbed the strength in my knees. Seeing her genuinely hurt drives my own anger right out of my system. I stutter and try to find the words to respond, but all I can come up with is; "I'm sorry."

"You got hurt and I couldn't protect you," she says, softer. She sniffles, and stray tears escape her eyes even as she scrunches up her face to hold them in. "I wasn't good enough."

I close the gap and hug her tightly. "You are good enough, we just weren't ready. You were right. I'm sorry, I should have listened to you and tried to work things out with Seath."

"I don't care about being right, I was just so scared when I saw you get hurt."

We hug for a moment more, parting to wipe the tears from our eyes. There is an awkwardness lingering in the air for a moment, until Cara speaks. "I didn't mean to yell. I'm not really mad at you."

"I know. Next time, we will do things better, okay? I promise I'll listen better, so please don't hide things from me," I tell her.

She nods and smiles. "It's a deal."

We continue on to the manor, where Seath is waiting outside by the tree, barefoot. He has his hand against the trunk and he seems to be whispering something. His sigil seems to be drained of its color—it looks like an old, faded tattoo. When he hears our footsteps, he lets out a sigh and looks towards us.

There is a pale green moth with a pink-trimmed edge along the forewings. It's vibrant and beautiful, and seems to linger around Seath for a moment before flying away.

We stop just before the tree, and Cara and I stand there awkwardly, studying Seath's stoic face. Cara nudges me, and I let out a quick sigh.

I know what she wants me to say, and the more I think about it, the more I think she may be right. I'm the one who lied to him. But on the other hand, he did overreact and yell. Surely, at the very least, we were both wrong. Shouldn't the onus to apologize be shared?

Then again, if one of us doesn't make the first move, neither of us will have the opportunity to make things right. I open my mouth to speak–

"Yukiko died in this house 30 years ago this December," Seath says gently, his gaze lost somewhere in the distance. "I buried her here, and planted a yew tree atop her grave, and every day I have tended to it." He runs a calloused hand down the tree, almost like a caress. "I was an orphan, and I kept to myself most of my life. I never really had a family or friends until I met her. She was the only person I have ever loved, and I only got to have her in my life for 12 short years."

He turns to look at me, then. "Time stopped for me the day she died. I spent 30 years alone in this house, waiting for the day my time would resume. And then it did, when you showed up."

"Why me?" I ask. The idea of inheriting Yukiko's powers comes back to my mind. The notion now feels heavy with the weight of both of their lives. I wonder what it is they hope I'll be able to do with Yukiko's power, if there is some kind of legacy I'm expected to fulfill.

"On the day she died, Yukiko told me that her heir would come one day, and she asked me to teach them so they could inherit her powers," he says. "She was one of the most powerful fortune tellers in the entire world, so there's no telling how much of this she predicted or if she had some sort of goal in mind, but the more I think about it, the more I can feel her hand still guiding us to our fates. You were meant to come here, Selena Amaris, and I was meant to teach you to become the next Witch of the Full Moon."

There is no way I can live up to her. Even the memory of her is intimidating. "But I don't understand why it's me and not someone else?"

"I don't know, either. Yukiko is the only one who can answer that question."

I look down at my feet. "I'm sorry for lying to you. What you asked me to do was reasonable, and I betrayed your trust."

He puts his hand on my shoulder. "I need you to be honest with your parents, and with me. I can't teach you otherwise."

"Help me tell them, then. Show them that magic is real."

Cara smiles. "I think that's a fair compromise, Seath. If you demonstrate your magic to Selena's parents and tell them that you're guiding us, they'll understand."

He nods his head. "Call them."

The entire time I am on the phone and subsequently waiting for them in the sitting room, my heart is pounding. I stand by the window, squirming as I watch the driveway, until the familiar blue hatchback finally pulls into the driveway, parking near Yukiko's tree.

Seath lets them into the house, guiding them to the sitting room where he has tea prepared. They make small talk, but I'm so anxious I can't focus.

Finally, Seath nods to me. It's time for honesty.

"Mr. and Mrs. Amaris, the reason I asked you to come out here today is because I learned last weekend that your daughter hasn't been entirely honest with you about how she spends her time here, and we want to make things right. I have no children of my own, but I know that if I had a young daughter, I would want to know when she's spending her time with an adult, and what she's doing in their home."

My dad nods meaningfully. "I appreciate you reaching out, but I'm a little confused. What is it exactly you're saying that you do here? It's my understanding that this is an afterschool club?"

Seath reaches for his teacup, deliberately holding it in the air before letting it drop. It shatters against the floor, the shards scattering across the hardwood.

My parents blink in surprise, Mom starting to ask, "What–?"

Without a word, Seath waves his hand in a small circle, and the pieces of the teacup begin to fly back together. It's like watching the shattering in reverse as it returns to its original shape. I watch as my parents stare in awe, their gazes moving from the teacup to Seath, who merely smiles at them before gesturing to the fireplace with a snap of his fingers, igniting the logs inside.

"Your daughter has been learning to perform magic. Not tricks like a magician, but honest to goodness magical spells."

My mom looks at me, then back at Seath in disbelief. "Magic?"

"Show them," Seath says, his gaze meeting mine.

I nod and walk over to the table, taking my grimoire from my backpack. My heart thumps in my chest, but I try to shake off my nerves. I open it to the fire spell, and cup my hands over the magic circle. A flame appears in my hand. I hold it up to my parents' awestruck faces, and they both reach out, recoiling when they feel the heat. I close my hands and the flame disappears. I then take out my cell phone and click Celly's app, and the phone starts to levitate around my left shoulder.

"Celly, meet Mom and Dad," I say nervously. "I accidentally used a spell meant to create a familiar to bring my phone to life. I named them Celly."

"Hello Rosalind, hello Jericho," Celly says.

"I prefer Jerry," my dad stammers awkwardly. "It's nice to meet you Celly."

"Call me Rosa," Mom adds. She looks at me, disbelief in her eyes. "This is real? This isn't some trick?"

"This is real," I say.

"This house and the magic I have both belonged to the former Mistress of this house, a woman named Elatha Yukiko," Seath explains. "She was known as the Witch of the Full Moon, and she was incredibly powerful. Your Selena has shown an affinity for the moon's magic, and I believe she has what it takes to inherit Yukiko's vast magical power. This means that your daughter will be able to change the world some day. Your daughter can become the next Witch of the Full Moon."

"Is this dangerous?" Mom asks breathlessly.

Seath nods. "If she uses her power recklessly and without guidance, it can be. But it is my intention to train her to be able to study and use magic safely. With my help, her exposure to magic—including some dangerous magic—can be controlled and supervised."

Dad turns to me. "How did you two even find this man?"

"Your daughter has prophetic visions in her dreams," Seath answers for me. "Yukiko had them, too."

"That's right. I had a dream about this house, and when I came here in person I found out the house was real, and Seath waiting for me," I add.

Seath lays a hand on my shoulder. "Yukiko predicted that her chosen heir would be drawn to this place one day, and that is Miss Selena. However, one of my conditions for me to train her is that she has your informed permission to do so. If you don't want her to learn, we can stop these lessons immediately. Miss Selena knows this."

"Do your parents know about this, Cara?" Mom asks.

Cara smiles. "They do. I showed my mom all the spells we've learned so far."

Mom takes a moment, presumably to think about what she will say next. The pausing gives me anxiety, and there is a silent tension in the air. "I don't like that you lied, and I don't want you doing things that are too dangerous. If there is a chance you could get hurt . . ."

"Not to scare you, but they have," Seath interjects. "By accident, Selena released a magic seal that kept five animal spirits inside. I intended to teach them how to collect these beings safely, but they were reckless and went after one of them last night in secret. Luckily, Miss Cara texted me and I was able to come and heal them."

Mom and Dad both share a combined expression of fear and disappointment. I can already predict their apprehensive response, but I speak up pre-emptively– "Things only got dangerous because I was being stupid. I lied to you and Seath, and I tried to do everything on my own, and that's why we got hurt. But I know I was wrong, and I won't do something like that again. Learning this stuff is important to me, it feels like this is what I was always supposed to be doing. I can't explain it, but there is this feeling in my chest like I belong here."

My parents look at each other, and Dad takes Mom's hand. They look into each other's eyes and seem to communicate without saying a single word to each other. Finally, Mom turns to look at me.

"Is this what you really want, honey?" she asks.

I nod. "It's been hard, but I love magic and I've never felt more alive."

There is a pregnant pause for what feels like an age, then–

"Alright, but you have to keep us informed from now on. No more hiding stuff, okay?" Mom says. "This is not a game. Take your safety seriously."

Dad adds, "And you're also grounded for lying to us, you know how we feel about that. No sleepovers with Cara for two weeks, and . . ." His voice trails off and he looks lost in thought. "I guess we can't exactly take your cellphone since it's alive now, isn't it?"

"Celly's pronouns are they/them," I say.

"Okay, well, um . . . No computer or video games for two weeks instead, then."

"Okay, Dad," I say with a smile.

Mom stares at Celly for a while. "Do we . . . feed them?"

"I do not require food," Celly responds. "I still require my battery to be charged for my smartphone features to be operable, and I still require a cellular or Wi-Fi connection to make calls, send messages, and access the internet. But my magically-granted capabilities, including my ability to speak and fly, do not use up any battery power as my lithium battery does not power magic."

Mom stands up and hugs me tightly. "Be safe, dear, please."

"I promise, Mom."

XI.

Crescent

I find myself standing at the base of a construction site. The skeleton of the building being assembled stands tall and bare before me. The earth is muddy and my shoes sink slightly with each step. I find myself walking down a path on the dirt lot toward the building. As I walk, the morning sun rises behind the structure, its rays almost blinding as they filter through the unfinished array of steel beams and wood scaffolding.

A massive eagle soars overhead, her wingspan easily passing 10 feet. She soars toward the sun, and following her with my eyes, I spot a stranger standing on one of the beams of the building, staring at me. I can't make them out, as the brightness of the sun effectively makes them little more than a silhouette, but something about them catches my focus.

I can't put my finger on what it is, but I feel some sort of kinship with them. As the brightness of the sun overwhelms my eyes, I turn away and find the giant eagle perched on top of a pile of wooden planks behind me.

She watches me intently, staring with her fiery, beady eyes.

I blink–

In an instant I am back in my bedroom. It's dark, and the shades are drawn over the window.

Ever since I met Seath I haven't had the dream about Yukiko. But this feels very similar. Seath said I have prophetic dreams—perhaps I should tell him about this one, too?

Last weekend I told my parents I could do magic. Now, today is the day Seath says I can finally become a true witch. I've been waiting all week for this. My whole life, really.

Celly flies over beside me. "Did you have a bad dream?"

"No, just a weird one. I think it was prophetic, somehow."

The dream remains on my mind for most of the morning as I get ready and leave to meet Cara, but by the time we arrive at Seath's home other things take precedence in my mind.

We gather in the library as usual. He drops a collection of different books from varying shelves on the main table, telling us which spells to copy over as he sits with a glass of amber liquid on the far side.

First and foremost is a spell we use immediately—Cara and I stand side by side, our hands over the new circles in our grimoires, and together we invoke them. The circles respond, and our books both glow for a moment as they become infused with a protective charm.

"Did it work?" I ask. Seath, without looking up, responds by flinging his drink onto the pages, but instead of staining or soaking into them, the liquid just splashes off harmlessly. Question answered, I suppose.

Next, I copy a spell we use to bind my grimoire to myself and Celly, allowing Celly to summon it or store it in a magical subspace when I'm not using it. To test it out, Celly raises their hand and the book begins to glow, then disappears. A second later, they make it reappear in the same spot.

I have Celly take notes for Cara and I as Seath lectures us. According to him, subspace is a layer of reality created by magic that is much more pliable, and as such, it is possible to create pockets in this subspace to achieve various effects. Powerful witches can go as far as trap people inside this subspace if they wish.

Seath teaches us a handful of other spells—a binding spell for subduing opponents, a spell for detecting magic at longer ranges, one for shielding oneself from physical attacks, and another spell for deflecting magic.

After a long day of copying the circles over to our grimoires and practicing with them, Seath stands up. He has asked us to stay late for the ritual, so we stay well past sunset, while he stands at the bay window watching the lake.

I excuse myself from the library and walk out to the water to try and mentally prepare myself for whatever is going to happen. The lake is still and reflects the rising moon with perfect clarity. The great pale globe peeks over the horizon, larger than life and further away than I could ever reach, just like Yukiko herself.

Seath said that being her successor meant I could change the world someday, but I don't even know where I'd begin. I'd like to help people with my magic, if I can, but I'm not even sure how.

I look back at the house, and I can see Seath in the window. He's looking at me as if seeing a ghost. I imagine Yukiko probably spent a lot of time out here while she was alive. I know I would, it's calm and beautiful. I wonder if she and I would have had much in common, or if we are entirely different. I wonder how much she knew about me, since she could see the future.

With one last look at the lake, I return to the study and Seath breaks his silence.

"The full moon is out now . . . it's time. Selena, come here."

He points to the center of the circle painted on the floor. I stand where he directs me, and look out of the bay window. The full moon looms large over the lake, and its image is intoxicating.

"Hold your hand out to the moon, and feel its power," Seath says quietly from my left. "Remember the cloud metaphor we talked about before? Use your cloud on the sigil below you. Activate it, then use it to draw the moon's power inside of you."

I follow his instruction. I reach out toward the silvery globe among the stars with my left hand, and despite its distance, I feel like I can almost touch it.

I can sense a vast world of power around me. The power to affect the tides, the power to commune with nocturnal animals, the power to connect to spirits, the power of a beacon to cut through the infinite darkness. It occurs to me that I never once questioned what it meant to be the Witch of the Full Moon. I never understood, but now it is starting to make sense.

The moon represents a vast celestial power that influences the very nature of the world. To command the moon means to control this nature. The moon does not represent darkness—it represents enduring light that breaks through darkness. It lights up the spiritual world in the way the sun lights up the physical one.

That was Yukiko. And is now me.

I feel like I am developing a deep and powerful understanding of the magic around me, and I become so lost in the feeling that I almost forget to engage the sigil.

Once I do, I can feel my skin grow cold. It's as if the library temperature dropped thirty degrees in an instant. I do as Seath instructed, and I try to draw the frigid, celestial power into my body, but the cold grows more intense, and a whirlwind of frosty air swirls around me, searing my skin with an icy chill.

Seath reaches his hand out and engages the circle with me. I can feel his magic joining mine, and helping to subdue the moon's might.

"As consort to the Moon's Mistress and arbiter of her will, I command thee, come to the hand of thy successor, Selena Amaris!" he shouts. His eyes lock onto me and he addresses me directly. "In the name of the witch Elatha Yukiko, I pass on her power to you! I declare you Selena Amaris, Witch of the Full Moon."

Ice forms on the back of my hand, drawing a circle. My whole body radiates a cool blue glow, and I am lifted from the ground by the winds. It feels both euphoric and agonizing all at once—the flow of the power is incredible, but my body shudders under the stress as if I will burst at any moment.

I scream, cathartically releasing some of the pain, and tears form in my eyes and turn to ice as they fall from my cheek. Something in me is warning me to stop, to cut off my magic and end the ritual here, but I am so close, I can feel it. I can become a true witch, if I just push a little harder.

I blink, and everything stops.

Time stands perfectly still, and the world around me looks fuzzy and unfocused, and standing before me is Yukiko herself, cold and elegant just as I remember from my dream.

"What's happening?" I ask her, wincing as my skin slowly freezes.

"You're not powerful enough to conquer the will of the Moon, so you are being rejected. It seems that you are not destined to become the Witch of the Full Moon at this time," she replies. "But you are too stubborn to give up."

"Does this mean I've failed?"

She nods. "But of course, you are only a child after all. You've only just begun to learn. A day will come when you realize your true potential, and when that day comes, you will have the power to claim my sigil as your own. But that doesn't mean you can't become a witch in the meantime."

"What?"

She touches my hand and the ice on it changes shape. "In my name as Witch of the Full Moon, I pass on a sliver of my power to you. I declare you, Selena Amaris, Witch of the Crescent Moon."

Time slowly starts to resume as Yukiko's frame turns to snow and disappears. Before she is gone completely, she walks right up to me, stepping on the empty air as if climbing invisible stairs, and whispers right in my ear, "If ever you are lost in the darkness, seek the light I have left within you."

She takes a step back and smiles. "Farewell moonchild," her voice echoes, though she is already gone.

My feet slowly touch back down, the winds slow and eventually disappear, and the light of the magic circle below me fades. The ice melts off of my skin, and the air around me quickly warms. I collapse to my knees, breathing heavily as my heart thumps loudly.

"Selena!" Cara calls, rushing over to me. She crouches down and touches my back.

"Are you hurt?" Celly asks, flying around to my front.

I shake my head. I don't feel hurt. Cara helps me to my feet and I look at Seath, who stares at me wide-eyed.

"Your hand . . ."

I look down and see it—where the ice was, a black crescent moon now lies, surrounded by a thick ring with geometric lines coming off of it.

"Why is it different?" Cara asks.

Seath walks over and takes my hand in his, inspecting it and tracing the circle with his fingertips. "You saw Yukiko, didn't you?"

I nod. "She said I wasn't ready yet, and gave me this sigil instead."

"A crescent moon?" Celly says, inspecting the symbol.

"Does this mean you're a witch now?" Cara asks.

I nod. "I am the Witch of the Crescent Moon."

XII.

Treasures

Tonight is the night we finally stop the raccoon thrall. As Cara and I stand outside the school gates, I run my fingers along the sigil on the back of my left hand. Celly floats at my side. Just this morning, as Seath was explaining the plan of attack, he also shared with me a spell to allow Celly to use other spells from my grimoire that I infuse them with.

I see Seath walking from the other side of the street as he finally arrives, flipping his hood down as he gets close. With his leather jacket he reminds me of what bikers look like in movies, so much so that I am tempted to ask him if he has a motorcycle. Something tells me he'd find the inquiry amusing.

"Is everyone ready?" he asks.

"Ready," Cara replies, her bow in hand. She is wearing a book strap over the cover of her grimoire, so that she can quickly retrieve and read from it mid-battle.

Celly's pixelated avatar salutes. "Ready, Seath!"

"I'm ready," I add. It's time to start fixing the damage I caused by releasing these thralls.

Celly lights the way as Seath leads us to the football field this time. Cara splits off from us, standing on the bleachers, while Celly flies a few meters away as well. Seath stays close to me. He nods to me, and just as we rehearsed earlier, I raise my branded fist to my chest then cast it out, scattering a fistful of magic dust ahead of us.

"Though thralls are magical, they are still animalistic. These pheromones will draw her to us."

As if on cue, the destroyed door's covering is torn off and the raccoon comes running in our direction.

"It's time I show you what I'm really capable of," Seath says.

He discards his leather jacket, then brings his hands together, interlocking his fingers then flipping them so his palms face out. He lets out a guttural growl and rips his hands away from each other, and in doing so, icy, bestial claws form on his hands, and his posture changes dramatically, a seething rage entering his eyes.

As the monster comes close we spring Seath's trap. Cara shoots the thrall in the abdomen with an arrow, and she predictably spins around to face her. Celly then flies in and bombards her with fireballs. Then, as she recoils, Seath rushes in and pulls her to her hindlegs with a stranglehold around her neck.

I run around to the front of the beast and raise my hand. I try to focus my energy on her, to penetrate her mind and compel her to relent and calm, to force her into a sealed form. The creature struggles, but for a moment, our eyes meet. I can sense a glimmer of recognition in her eyes before it quickly changes to confusion and rage.

Suddenly she thrashes, pushing Seath off and running at me. Cara fires another arrow that sinks into her shoulder, but she doesn't slow down. Instinctively I raise my hands and shriek, and the raccoon crashes into an invisible, frosty wall separating us.

"Selena!" Seath roars as he rushes in, grabbing the massive creature and dragging her back from my barrier. They begin trading blows with their claws, narrowly avoiding cutting into each other.

Celly comes to my side with Cara in tow. "What do we do?" Cara asks. "I can't risk shooting an arrow when they're so close, I might hit Seath by mistake."

I think for a moment. I look up at the stars. They are like tiny glowing snowflakes dotting the sky. They remind me of something Seath once said about magic.

Magic is the art of applying will to imagination to influence the world.

I raise my hand. The stars must have some connection to the moon, as they are only visible when the moon is. Though I'm not certain of how sound my logic is, I feel it's enough to apply my own imagination.

Half a dozen stars turn into beams of light that rain down from the sky, hitting the raccoon all at once and freezing everything they touch. She tries to claw herself out of the ice, but Cara shoots one shoulder and Seath slashes the other, disabling both arms.

I focus once more on getting the creature to submit. I feel connected to her through our magic, and try to manipulate that bond to settle her mind, spiritually calling for her to calm down. I can feel the confusion and fear in her mind, and wordlessly I exert my influence on our connection to compel her to be still.

98

The raccoon struggles against the ice for another moment, then she relents.

The ethereal body of the beast becomes luminescent, and a sense of calm washes over us both. She closes her eyes just as I close my hand, and the beast fades away. When I reopen my hand, a little, clear, aqua-colored stone is there in the shape of a raccoon.

Cara, Celly, and Seath all gather around. Seath dismisses his claws and takes the stone.

"Yukiko is gone, my old friend," he whispers to the stone. "It's time you go, too. Rest now."

The stone glows and then turns to dust in his hands. As it scatters to the wind I can't help but notice his sigil has faded even further.

"What did you do?" Celly asks.

"I let her go. The thralls are acting out because they don't understand why they can't hear or sense Yukiko anymore. They're scared, and confused, and don't know what to do. Once we subdue them, I can dismiss their spirits and allow them to pass on with her."

Cara looks at me carefully. "How did you do that? With the stars and the ice and stuff?"

"I don't know, I just imagined it," I reply.

"You're a witch, this is what your power is now," Seath says.

At that moment, a gust of wind tears through the field, kicking up dust and unveiling a huge pile of stuff by the far goal post.

"What is that?" I say, walking over.

Cara approaches the haphazard pile of books, clothes, trophies, instruments, and other items. She kneels down and picks up a bundle of photos. "It's everything that went missing from the school."

"Raccoons are thieves and scavengers, after all. Without any direction from Yukiko, she must have naturally sought to steal every precious item from the school for safe-keeping," Seath explains.

"These items are precious?" Celly asks.

Seath shrugs, retrieving Wulfflæd's book from the pile and dusting it off. "What's precious is subjective. Different people consider different things treasures."

Atop a pile of discarded designer clothes I see a familiar book, its dark stormy cover almost hidden completely.

As I pick it up, Celly comes over and observes it. "What makes this your treasure, Selena?"

I look back at Cara, who is smiling to herself as she thumbs through photos of us from over the years we've known each other. "It's not, it's what it says inside."

I open the cover to reveal a penned message.

> *Happy 14th birthday Selena! I remember you said you wanted this book back in March so I picked it up that weekend. I've held on to it all year just to give it to you today. I just wanted to tell you thank you. I know that I'll never be alone because you will always be my friend. And no matter what, I will always be there for you!*

XIII.

The Sun's Omen

With the items mysteriously returned, the school's investigation into the break-in ceased. Thanks to Seath, they never found out about the cafeteria or the football field being trashed, so the whole case was chalked up to an instance of vandalism and life moved on. Luckily, not too many people asked about my sigil, and Cara intervened to tell those who did inquire that it was just a tattoo.

As I walk to school on a particularly chilly Monday morning, I can't help but think how crazy things have been. In a matter of a few weeks I discovered magic was real, became a witch, and defeated a thrall. It's been a month since the fight, and while we have not seen any signs of the other four, our lessons with Seath have carried on. It occurs to me that my birthday is only a week away now.

"Celly?" I say, holding them so they don't attract attention from strangers.

"Yes, Selena?"

"Do you have a birthday?"

Celly appears to think for a minute. "I don't believe I do."

"Would you like one? Every human has a birthday—even animals have them."

"I think I'd like that. When would my birthday be?"

That's a tough question. The day the phone was made? That doesn't feel right. There was no sense of personality or any kind of bond then. "The way I see it, you have two options. Either the day I first took you home, or the day I gave you magic powers."

"The day you took me home, then. I think that has to be the most important day in my life."

"April first, last year, then. You're a whole one year old, Celly."

I see Cara by the school gate waiting for me as usual. I wave to her and quicken my pace, and we greet each other. It really does feel like life has settled down—though in the back of my mind I know that the raccoon thrall was only the first of five. The wolf is still out there, along with the bat, skunk, and owl.

Cara and I go to our morning class and take our seats, and the teacher comes in, leaving the door ajar. From my desk I can just barely make out the shadow of another person in the hall.

"Attention everyone, this morning we have a new student joining us! His parents just moved here from Hawai'i. Allow me to introduce Kiran Hoku. Come on in here, Kiran!"

The boy is fit and tall, with short, thick black curls and dark eyes with telltale circles under them revealing him to be the type of person who stays up late. He is evidently not quite used to the cold as he bundles up under two black hoodies with long gray hand-made fingerless gloves and faded, loose-fitting gray jeans. There is something intense about his gaze as he looks around with his narrow, reddish-brown eyes.

"Introduce yourself," the teacher nudges.

The boy looks uncomfortable, but he says, "I'm Kiran, I used to live in Hawai'i with my parents, then for a while I stayed in Florida, and now I'm staying here. My family moves a lot for work. I was on the baseball team at my old school, and I have a golden doodle dog. I can't think of anything else to say, thank you."

Everyone claps as their default, dispassionate response, and Kiran is ushered into the empty desk in the back row opposite the room from me.

Something about him feels warm, yet odd. I constantly feel like his eyes are on me, but every time I look back he's focused on his textbook or looking forward, a bored and sleepy expression on his face. Over the course of class I look back at least half a dozen times, but not once do I catch him looking at me. Still, I can't shake the feeling.

He ends up being in my second class of the day as well, seated two rows in front of me. The entire class I can hardly focus. My eyes keep looking in his direction, though he doesn't look back once.

At lunch, Cara and I go outside to eat our sandwiches on the bleachers. I take Celly out and lay them flat so they can join us.

"Have you talked to the new boy yet?" Cara asks.

"What new boy?" Celly says.

"There's a new student from Hawai'i. I haven't talked to him, but I got kind of a weird vibe from him."

Cara's eyes narrow suspiciously. "What kind of vibe?"

"I don't know, I felt like he was staring at me, but every time I looked he wasn't," I say. "I got the same sense in my next class even though I sat behind him, so I know for a fact he never once turned around. It's weird."

Suddenly, the feeling comes back to me, intensely enough that the hairs on the back of my neck stand up. I look around and see nothing for a moment, but then there he is, walking along the bottom of the bleachers, seemingly unaware of our presence.

But something is strange—how did he get so close to us without either of us noticing? How did I not see him at first when I looked around?

Finally, he notices us and waves politely, walking up to us.

"Hello, you're in my first period class," he says to Cara, then turns to me. "And you're in both of my morning classes, right?"

Cara smiles. "That's right. Your name is Kiran?"

He nods. "Is it alright if I ask your names? I don't really know anyone here yet."

"I'm Selena," I say, trying to be polite.

"And I'm Cara Philomena. I've at least looked at almost every club in the school, and I'm in the cooking club, the anime club, the book club, the school paper, and the girls volleyball team, so if you want suggestions, you can ask me."

Kiran shakes his head. "That's alright. I play baseball, but the season is already over. If I'm still here next semester, I'll go to tryouts for that."

He looks down at my hand and frowns at my sigil for a moment, before his face softens up again. "That's a cool tattoo, what does it mean?"

"Oh, it doesn't mean anything, I just uhh . . . really like the moon," I lie.

He nods meaningfully. "I'm sorry for interrupting your lunch, it was nice meeting you two. I hope I'll see you around."

As he walks away I notice an eagle, like the one from my dream, perched on the school roof. Do eagles migrate in the winter? I pick up Celly to Google it and the answer is 'sometimes'. Still, it feels oddly out of place. I've never seen a bird like that around here.

I can't help but notice that Kiran is in my next class, as well as our last class of the day, gym.

Cara has club activities today so I walk home by myself. On the way, I find myself on a empty street. I look around to make sure I am completely alone, then, just for practice, I hold out my left fist, focus for a moment, and then open it, creating one of Seath's fairy lights in my open palm. I lower my hand, dismissing the magic.

I look around one last time, just to be sure—only to see Kiran at the edge of the street.

My heart skips a beat. Did he see me do that? But it seems like he isn't paying attention. He hasn't even noticed me and he is turning down a different street. Perhaps I'm just being paranoid.

As I start walking back home, the shadow of an eagle passes by, but when I look up I can't see the bird.

XIV.
Footprints in the Snow

"You're in danger," the voice whispers.

I find myself back in the construction site dream. I hear the silky voice whisper it again, but I cannot find the source.

I look back at the silhouette standing in the frame of the building, but I still can't make out any details. The sun behind them grows bigger and bigger, seemingly consuming the world.

My heart starts to race in my chest and my breathing grows shallow and rapid.

"You need to escape," the voice echoes.

The sun grows larger, consuming the building itself, and expanding toward me. As I turn to run, the eagle is right in front of me, flying fast and poised to attack. I fall backward in surprise as it passes over my head, and when I turn, the sun is upon me.

I open my mouth to scream—

I wake suddenly, back in my bed, shooting straight up.

I struggle to find my breath, wheezing and gasping for a few unsettling moments. Despite it being chilly, I am caked in sweat and my skin feels hot to the touch. My hands are shaking and I anxiously look around to confirm that I'm safe in my bed.

It takes a moment, but I find myself slowly returning to reality. Once my breathing returns to normal, I realize that my throat is scratchy and dry.

Maybe I should have told Seath about the dream after all. I check Celly—it's 4:36 in the morning, and I have an outstanding text from Cara sent at 12:01 that reads 'Happy birthday bestie! I hope your day is as magical as you are!' with a bunch of moon emojis. I smile to myself, but I decide not to respond yet. I know Cara takes her phone off silent mode at nights so that if there's an emergency text the ringer will wake her.

I get out of bed and walk down to the kitchen, getting myself a glass from the cupboard beside the sink and pouring some ice water from the fridge. I lean against the island counter and absentmindedly sip the water.

I hold open my palm and create a single fairy light. If I focus, I can change its color. I settle on a vibrant violet that fills the room. I pluck an ice cube from my glass and hold it up to the light, and it sparkles brilliantly through the ice's imperfections.

"That's beautiful," a voice calls from the entryway. I look over my shoulder, and see Mom leaning against the doorframe. "Happy birthday, Gummybear."

I smile at her. "I hate that nickname."

"I know," she says sweetly, walking in and leaning against the countertop across from me. "Do you know why I call you that?"

"Dad says it's the only thing you wanted to eat when you were pregnant with me."

She nods, laughing quietly to herself.

We stand in silence for a few minutes, both of us just watching the light. I make it move off to the side so that it is not between us, and I make it shift to an orangey-red.

"I'm proud of you, Selena."

"Mom," I huff, rolling my eyes.

"Listen to me," she says firmly. The sudden sharpness in her voice catches me off guard, and I look at her, studying her expression. It's a mix of warmth and anxiousness.

She fidgets with her hands for a moment, then lets out a deep exhale. "I want you to know that I am proud of you. I always knew you would do incredible things, and now you can do this–" She gestures to the light. "You're growing up into a talented, unique, special young woman, and I love you."

I don't know what to say. I know that it means a lot to her to be able to say these things. I know that I should say something. But the words won't come. It feels awkward to vocalize the feeling I have in the pit of my heart.

What if I say the wrong thing? Or say things in the wrong way? What do I even tell her? 'I love you too'? That feels cheesy and far too sappy. Do we even have that kind of relationship? Saying it offhand, or using it as a sign off for a text feels much less serious, much easier to say.

Noticing my awkwardness, she walks around the island, taking my hands. She looks sad for some reason—perhaps she's upset that I couldn't think of what to say?

"Are you okay?" I ask.

She nods. "Your magic is the first thing you've ever kept from me. And I'm not mad, but it made me realize you're not a little girl anymore. I know you're getting to be more independent, but I just want you to know that no matter how old you get I will always be here for you, okay? You never outgrow your mom."

"I know, Mom," I say, my throat suspiciously tight. "I'm sorry I didn't tell you."

"I kept worse things from my mom, I understand," she says, reaching out and wrapping me in a tight hug. "I just want to make sure you know that you can always trust me, and you can always talk to me. I'll always be on your team."

I wrap my arms around her. "Thank you, Mom."

She takes one last look at me as we part, before smiling and saying, "Happy birthday."

I linger in the kitchen for a while after she leaves, waking up Celly for company.

Eventually, I return to bed for the precious last few moments of sleep before I have to wake up for school. The school day itself seems to fly by. I still can't shake the feeling that the new student, Kiran, is watching me, but Cara keeps me distracted as we talk and gossip the hours away. After school, Cara skips her club activities to walk home with me and celebrate my birthday. She reveals a big, narrow box that she stashed in her locker before I arrived, wrapped neatly in purple paper with a lavender bow.

We get to my house and Dad is waiting there in the—now messy—kitchen, proudly displaying a homemade cake sloppily decorated with purple frosting and fifteen candles. Mom offers us both a cup of tea and a spread of vegan appetizers she prepared for us. I wake Celly to join us in celebrating, too.

We have an early dinner gorging on apps and snack foods until it is time for us to gather around the cake. Cara ignites the candles with a spell, and I blow them out, wishing most of all to have more moments like these—where everyone is happy.

Mom cuts up Dad's cake and passes out the pieces. It's delicious despite the amateur presentation.

Finally, it comes time for presents. We sit around the living room and everyone brings their gift boxes to me. Dad gifts me a brand new drawing tablet that I can use with my computer. It's high-end and practical, and I love it. My mom gives me a hand-knit black scarf for the cold weather coming up, and a moon-shaped locket with a family photo inside.

Cara hands me her box next. "Once we started to learn magic, I knew that this was what I was going to do for your birthday. I spent a lot of late hours after school working on it so that it'd be ready on time."

I open the box, and inside is a hand-sewn outfit.

"Try it on!" she urges.

I slip away to the bathroom under the stairs to change, and that's when I realize what it really is she made. The black, pointed witch hat with the purple bow fits snugly on my head. There is a purple dress with a black belt, black leggings, and knee-high black boots, and the final piece of the ensemble—a black cloak with purple trim going overtop everything else.

I walk back into the living room in awe, and everyone stares as I do.

"Cara . . . this is so beautiful!" I choke out, almost moved to tears.

She smiles politely. "You're a true witch now, so I thought you should look the part. After all, you should always dress for the occasion."

"It feels magical," I say, inspecting myself. Something about it makes me feel more in tune with my sigil and with the moon itself.

There is a knock at the door, and I can instantly tell— "It's Seath."

As Dad goes to answer the door, Celly flies over with a smile on their avatar, taking photos of me from different angles. "I thought you'd like to remember this moment!"

"I would, thank you. Come here, Cara!" I pull her to her feet to pose with me.

As we finish up with photos, Seath walks into the room. He towers over everyone else, having to bend his neck to avoid hitting the door frame with his head.

"Happy birthday, kiddo," he says awkwardly. "I have something for you."

I walk up to him, and he stares at me for a moment, until I start to feel self-conscious.

"Sorry," he says. "You just . . . you look like a proper witch now, Selena of the Crescent Moon."

He takes out a little box and shows it to me. I open it, revealing a silver ring featuring a crescent moon cradling a beautiful blue topaz stone.

"This belonged to Yukiko. I think there is only one person on this earth she would ever share it with, and that person is you. It is enchanted, though I don't actually know what spell it is or what it does."

I take it out and slip it on my left ring finger. It's cool to the touch and sparkles brilliantly in the light. "It's gorgeous, Seath, thank you."

"Yukiko would have really liked you, I think. You two would have gotten along like peas in a pod."

"It looks like an engagement ring," Cara comments. "Did you give it to her?"

Seath chuckles. "I did give her a ring, once, but the one I gave her is still on her finger. I'm afraid you won't ever get your hands on that one, that's all hers. This one she already had when we met. She said it was a gift, though she never told me who it was from."

I can feel the magic inside the ring, but it feels different from the powers of the moon. There's something else present, something warm, deep within. Someone very powerful must have made this.

XV.

Blade of the Sun

I stand at the shore of Falling Star Lake, a strange magic circle drawn into the dirt around me with a dreamcatcher array surrounded by a thick ring. Seath, Cara, and Celly face me, just outside of the circle.

"This is the dream spell. It will allow me to see your dreams. I think that if I can see them, I can help you to interpret them," Seath says, his own leather-bound black grimoire in his hand.

"On the count of three, both of you will invoke the circle at the same time—Selena will recall her dream and Seath will enter it, just like instructed," Celly says.

I close my eyes and await the countdown.

"3 . . . 2 . . . 1 . . ."

Seath and I both activate the spell at the same time, and I find myself standing at his side in the construction site.

Just like always, the sun is blazing, causing the person in the building to be silhouetted and impossible to make out.

"I know this place. I pass by it whenever I go downtown," he says.

The eagle flies overhead and lands on a nearby lumber pile, staring us down. As Seath sees her, he instinctively grabs my arm and stands between us. His grip is hard enough that it hurts, but I dare not say anything when I see the intensity on his face. I notice that he has deliberately grabbed me with his right hand, leaving his sigil free to cast.

"Cyra Oralie," he growls.

The eagle flies off toward the sun, and suddenly it is night and where the silhouetted figure once stood is a large four-foot bat dangling from the beam upside down. A crescent moon fills the sky where the sun once was, and the intense warmth is replaced by a comforting chill.

My eyes open and I am back on the shore with Cara and Celly. Seath stumbles, and Cara and I both rush to either side to try and hold him up.

"Are you okay?" Cara asks.

Celly flies in close. "Should I dial 911?"

"You can do that on your own?" Seath asks wearily. "You're mighty useful, Celly."

He steadies himself and gently steps away from us. "I'm alright, girls. Dream-reading magic is incredibly powerful, it just took a lot out of me. I just need to nap for a bit and I'll be okay. The thrall bat is at that construction site on Renly Boulevard. That's why you've been dreaming of that place. We can go tomorrow."

He slowly walks past us toward the house. I can't help but observe that his sigil is barely noticeable now, having lost almost all of its vibrancy.

"Who's Cyra Oralie?" I call.

He stops, and his fists clench. Without turning back, he says, "The Witch of the Sun."

As he leaves our view, Celly floats closer to Cara and I. "I believe that spell was more harmful to Seath than he led on. I can sense his vitality, and he is severely weakened."

"Then we should go and deal with the bat ourselves," I say.

Cara nods. "We've learned from our fight with the raccoon thrall. We won't make the same mistakes again."

Reasoning that even at night the city will be busy, Cara and I plan to have a sleepover at my house, and we wait until midnight to sneak out. I wear the outfit Cara made, and we ride our bikes through the streets, following Celly's directions until we reach the construction site, walled off by fences lined with plywood. We park our bikes at the main entrance, and Cara approaches the chain that is wrapped around the gate and the fencepost, and padlocked to seal it shut.

Cara opens her grimoire and creates a small, hot flame and aims it at one link in the chain until it turns red, then white. The texture of the steel becomes soft and the chainlink starts to lose its shape.

Cara and I nod to each other, and I reach out my hand and manipulate the winds to pull the chain in opposite directions until the hot link snaps in half, allowing us entry. The path leading to the building skeleton is exactly like my dream, and when we approach, I half expect to see the giant bat sitting right where I saw it perched this morning, but there is nothing.

But I can sense something. I feel a magical presence moving with the winds.

Cara retrieves her bow. "I hear something . . . it sounds like wings?"

I feel an intense sense of dread in my chest, so much so that it leaves me weak in the knees, then all of the sudden some invisible force strikes me in the chest, pushing me down.

"Selena! What just happened?" Cara calls from the ground beside me.

Celly flies in close. "I believe the thrall is invisible."

"Well that's just cheating!" Cara whines, looking around. An invisible force clamps down on her arm as I climb back to my feet, and it tosses her bow away from her.

Suddenly, a gust of wind pushes us both over, and we help each other stand again.

"What do we do?" I ask frantically, looking around and trying to follow the monster with my senses.

"I have an idea!" Cara replies, looking out towards the building itself. She runs, and I put up a barrier around my whole body.

Immediately I feel sharp claws scrape my barrier, and I spin around and raise my sigil, casting a concentrated burst of wind from my palm. I react with another blast each time the barrier is struck, but I'm unable to hit the creature.

Finally, the barrier is broken and I feel a clawed foot grab the chest of my dress and shove me down to the ground. Suddenly, a snow-white splash of paint hits the invisible creature, revealing its form to us.

Celly immediately blasts the bat with fire, knocking her back and causing her invisibility to wear off.

"Great work! Now restrain her!" I shout.

Cara uses the binding spell, creating a series of magical threads that wrap around the bat and hold her down. I raise my hand to try and force her to calm like before, but she fights against the binds and refuses to let me in.

Suddenly, she lets out a loud, high-pitched screech that hurts so much that I can't focus or think.

When the screech finally ends, my head is pounding and I feel like my ears are going to bleed. I try to get my bearings, but the bat grabs me by the shoulders and takes off into the air. Cara has been pushed to the ground, too, and as she scrambles to get up and run for her bow, Celly follows me.

"I can't shoot any fire," Celly calls. "I might hit you!"

I struggle against the bat, but she takes me almost thirty feet into the air.

For a moment I feel like I'm back in the dream, and when I look, there is a figure standing on the beams of the unfinished structure, though I can't make them out in the shadows. They raise their hand and six streaks of light shoot off in random directions then curve back around to strike the bat, igniting her. She drops me, and I scream as I fall toward the ground, but the figure raises their hand and disappears, and at that exact second I am caught as they reappear beside me and wrap their arms around me, landing us softly on the ground.

That is when I get a good look at their face and see that it's—

"Kiran?!"

"Focus!" he commands, setting me down. "I'll restrain the thrall."

His left hand is uncovered, revealing an elaborate symbol that looks like a sun on the back of his hand. Fiery tendrils erupt from the earth and fly up to grab the bat and drag her to the ground, holding her. As she opens her mouth to screech again, Kiran creates a crystalline barrier around her so the sound can't escape.

I can sense the rage inside the bat, as well as the fear. She feels abandoned and doesn't understand why Yukiko won't come for her.

"It's okay," I coo, stepping toward the creature, slow and steady. She calms and looks directly at me. "Yukiko hasn't abandoned you. She's waiting for you to come to her. You don't have to fight anymore."

The bat fades away and becomes a small aqua stone sharing her likeness.

Cara and Celly both come to my side, and I look back at Kiran.

"He can use magic, that's why you felt weird about him," Cara says, standing between him and I protectively. "You were sensing his magical powers."

"But boys can't use magic," I say, recalling Seath's lessons. "So that must mean you're–"

"That's right," Kiran interrupts. "Allow me to introduce myself properly. I am Kiran of the Hoku family, Vassal to the Witch of the Sun, Cyra Oralie."

XVI.

Sigil of the Sun

"What are you doing here?" I ask Kiran.

He stares me down. "I could ask you the same question. Who are you? There are no known witches in this area, I was not told of any magical beings aside from the thralls, but your presence is huge and you're not even trying to hide it!"

"We're trying to find all the thralls," Celly says.

"What is that thing?" he replies, watching Celly in utter befuddlement. The sounds of sirens fill the air and Kiran's eyes lock toward the gate. "We have to go, we'll continue this talk at school on Monday!"

Before I can say anything else, he rushes off toward the building, disappearing.

"We should run, too," Cara says.

We make our way to the side and scale the fence together with Celly flying overhead to keep watch. We trace the wall back around to the front, where two police cars are parked and the gate is open. We make a run for our bikes and ride them home as fast as we can.

In the morning, we go back to Seath's home to return the bat stone and talk about Kiran, but he isn't there. Cara tries to text him but he doesn't reply, and he doesn't show up even after an hour of waiting. At a loss for what to do, we return home, anxious to see Kiran the next day.

Monday morning, I meet up with Cara at the front of the school. We say nothing, but we stay on our guard. Kiran comes to class acting totally normal, ignoring us right until the lunch bell, when he gets up to greet me.

"Let's talk," he says, a grim expression on his face.

Cara is not in our second period class. Instead, she meets us at the back doors of the school, and from there we walk to the bleachers.

It's a chilly day, even with our coats on the wind makes it very cold. The upside is that no one but us is outside, so I can safely wake Celly up. Cara and I sit side by side as Kiran stands in front of us and removes his left glove.

"Who are you really?" I ask apprehensively.

"I told you exactly who I was last night. It's time for you to answer some questions. For there to be a witch that Mistress Oralie didn't know about is serious," he declares.

Oralie, as in Cyra Oralie—the Witch of the Sun. "I don't even know who that is!" I reply, which is technically true. Seath didn't say anything about her beyond her name, but he definitely didn't like her.

Cara studies Kiran for a moment. "Before anything, how do we know we can trust you? If you can answer that, then we'll talk."

Kiran nods. "That's reasonable. I suppose I could start by saying I'm not here to fight you or interfere with you at all, I'm only here to make sure the thralls don't hurt anyone while they're running wild. If you don't know who Cyra Oralie is, then you probably don't know much about the magical community in general. Cyra Oralie is the Witch of the Sun, and she protects other witches like you by carefully monitoring how magic is used all over the world and keeping track of magical people. She detected powerful magic coming from this town and sent me to investigate, and when I got here, I sensed your magical presence. I promise I'm only here to keep people safe."

Cara and I share a glance, and she nods. I can sense that he's being honest with me, and I get the same sense I felt when I first met Seath as well—this feels like someone I can trust.

"The thralls aren't mine," I tell him. "We're trying to stop them too, we don't want anyone to get hurt. We only started learning magic in September, Cara is a spellcaster and I only just became a full witch at the beginning of October."

"Counting the bat thrall we defeated, there are three more remaining in the city," Celly adds.

Kiran looks at Celly and points. "What is that, anyways, and why is it alive?"

"That phrasing is a little rude, but Celly is Selena's familiar," Cara answers. "Their pronouns are they and them, please don't call them 'it'."

"I didn't know that was possible," he replies, gazing at Celly inquisitively before turning his attention back to me. "So if you're a new witch, how are you learning to use magic? What's your title?"

"I'm the Witch of the Crescent Moon," I say, pride swelling in my chest. "I have a teacher, he used to be the consort of a witch who isn't alive anymore. Those thralls were created by her and sealed away, and I accidentally woke them up, so he's training me to use magic so I can collect them."

"It seems like we're all after the same thing, so why don't we work together?" Cara says, standing up. "Kiran, you seem more experienced with magic, and Selena, Celly, and I obviously can't do this alone."

Kiran extends his hand, and Cara shakes it. "I should meet this teacher of yours."

After lunch, we continue our day as normal, but as soon as school ends, we all meet up by the entrance and walk over to Seath's home.

As we make our way up the driveway, Kiran noticeably tenses up in his shoulders, taking his gloves off. Something about the house that seems so warm and inviting to me appears to be making him anxious.

We walk up to the house, and I feel a strange sensation— like someone around us has suddenly become enraged. I can feel animosity in the air, and it makes me nervous as I approach the steps.

Just as we pass the yew tree, I get a sickening chill up my spine, and Cara and I both spin around to find Seath with his magic claw wrapped around Kiran's neck from behind.

"Try something, boy," Seath growls. "Watch what happens."

"Seath!" Cara shrieks.

"What are you doing?" I yell out.

"You girls don't understand, that sigil–"

"It's the Sigil of the Sun!" I interrupt, stepping closer. "He told us!"

Seath scowls. "Did he also tell you that his mistress, Cyra Oralie, tried to kill Yukiko?"

"Elatha Yukiko?" Kiran blurts out. "The Witch of the Full Moon? But then . . . you must be that Seath, Yukiko's mad dog!" He looks to us. "This man is your teacher?"

"Everyone stop and explain what's going on!" Cara shouts. "We don't know your history, maybe you two have good reasons to be angry, but we don't know what they are and this isn't going to solve anything!"

"He saved us when we fought the bat thrall! We would have gotten hurt," I say, placing my hand on Seath's arm. I can sense my touch alleviating his anger. His posture softens, but he remains tense and aggressive.

His eyes flick to me. "You don't know Cyra like I do, if he's serving her, he's dangerous."

"I can't explain why, but I know that Kiran is good. I can feel it in my heart, we don't have to be scared of him."

Seath's claws disappear and he relaxes—slightly. Kiran breathes a sigh of relief, and Seath gestures for us all to follow him inside. We sit around the fireplace as Seath stands at its side, listening to Cara explain what Kiran told us. Seath glances at me and keeps his arms crossed.

Once she finishes, there is a heavy silence in the air. I'm not sure what to think or say. "So clearly Cyra and Yukiko didn't get along," I say finally.

"There was a time when they were inseparable," Seath explains, letting out a loud sigh. "Many years ago they were very close indeed, and they did many amazing things together, but something happened that caused them to turn against each other."

"What was it?" Celly asks from my shoulder.

Seath shakes his head. "It's complicated. But by the time I met Yukiko their companionship was already long-since dissolved. They were opposed to each other, and fought many battles during my time with her, and even now, decades later, I can recall the pain she went through in her efforts to defeat Cyra."

"We were always told Yukiko was the aggressor, that she betrayed Cyra and that's why they fought," Kiran says, lifting his chin.

"You don't know a damn thing! I was there," Seath growls through gritted teeth.

"Well you were there after the fact," Cara notes.

"Does any of this matter anymore, though?" I ask. "Yukiko is gone, and Kiran had nothing to do with that conflict."

"He still works for Cyra, and that means I can't trust him," Seath says. "I will never forgive her, and I will not let go of all the things she did."

"Look, the only thing I was sent here to do is deal with the thralls. I don't want to fight with anyone and Cyra is busy with another investigation," Kiran says. "Cara was right when she said we should work together. I'm here on good faith."

"I have a question," Celly says, stroking their chin. "How is it Cyra could detect the thralls but not any of us?"

"I imagine there are powerful protective charms in place to protect against all kinds of divination magic," Kiran says. "Yukiko's talents were legendary, after all."

To that, Seath grins. "That's correct, the house itself is infused with hundreds of spells that effectively cloak the magical presences of people under the jurisdiction of the moon . . . among other things."

"So as long as Kiran says nothing, Cyra won't know about me? About us?" I say.

Kiran nods. "It seems that way. She certainly didn't know about you before she sent me, and she has powerful divination magic at her command."

"Give us your word that you will say nothing, then," Seath says, bringing his grimoire out, opening it on the table. "Swear it."

The circle on the page is a wheel, with an eye shape at the center of its spokes. The pupil is a black spikey dot that for some reason feels unnerving. Seath stretches his open hand over the circle. Kiran hesitates, but finally he extends his, and they clasp hands tightly.

They invoke the circle at the same time, and a thousand needles appear around Kiran. I jump back in my seat, but they both seem calm. He clears his throat. "I vow to say nothing of Selena, Cara, this house, or yourself to Cyra Oralie, for so long as this bond remains."

As they part, the needles disappear, and Kiran is left inspecting his hand.

"Wha – " Cara begins.

"The short version is, if he breaks his promise he'll be stabbed by a thousand needles," Seath explains, anticipating her question. "Okay, I agree to this, boy. There are three more thralls to collect, so let's find them."

XVII.

December

Seath leads us on this chilly Friday afternoon to the woods north of town, to a clearing off a beaten hiking trail, ankle-deep in the first heavy snowfall of the season. Kiran trudges along ahead of Cara, Celly, and I, his teeth chattering as he curses the weather under his breath.

Kiran has opted to share some of the magic circles in his grimoire, with Seath's blessing.

Seath stands back, arms crossed, observing with Celly by his shoulder. Kiran first gives Cara two spells to copy into her book, and as she does, he raises his hand and suspends three flat discs of soft mud in the air.

"Try them out," he says.

She nods, placing her open grimoire on the ground beside her, then she takes her bow in hand. She invokes the first spell, draws an arrow, and shoots into the heart of one of the mud targets. Upon impact the arrow releases a flurry of flames that ignite the target. She fires at the other targets with similar results.

I can feel her smiling even while her back is to me. Aside from its potency, the spell also looks really fun to use. It almost makes me regret not learning archery with her.

She invokes the second spell he passed on to her, and this time on impact the arrow releases a shockwave of lightning that shatters the target into little pieces.

Kiran creates more targets for her, then wanders away from Cara's makeshift shooting range. He waves to me, and I walk over to him, wondering what he has in store for me.

"Here, this is the lightning blade spell," he gestures to the circle. I copy it over, and he steps back, nodding to me.

"What will it do," I ask cautiously.

"It's all in the name. It's a blade. Made out of lightning. I don't really know how else to explain it," he says.

Descriptive. Well, I guess there's no use trying to get him to tell me more when I can just try it out myself. Kiran raises his fist to his hip, then swings it out as if he's holding something, then he gestures for me to copy the motion.

I follow along with him as I invoke the spell, and in a flash a blade of lightning appears in my grip, shocking everything it touches except for myself. It feels weird. It doesn't feel like it should have weight, but it does—it's not heavy, per se, but it certainly generates momentum when I swing. Every part of the sword, even the hilt, is made out of lightning. It sparks and arcs inside itself, holding its curved shape perfectly, and when I swing it hard enough, arcs shoot out and burn things in front of me. I find it hard to control, and far more tactile than most of the spells I am used to.

Kiran's usage of magic feels much more physical and direct than the spells I have become accustomed to.

After some practice, I open my hand to release the blade and it disappears. I'm ready to learn the next spell he has planned for me.

He shows me one more circle to copy. "This will enhance your physical abilities in short bursts."

I nod and invoke it, and this feeling of raw power explodes inside my body, and with it a sense of energy and euphoria. I test it out, jumping much higher than natural, and sprinting faster than world-record pace. Cara even stops what she's doing to watch in wonder. It feels amazing, and I can't help but be giddy as I experiment with the spell.

Finally, to test the strength I've been imbued with, I find a massive fallen tree by the clearing's edge. I lift the entire thing over my head with little strain. It still *feels* heavy, but it's manageable.

Cara and Celly both clap at my feat of strength, and Kiran praises how well I adapt to the spell. Seath watches on with a look of pride.

As the sun starts to set, we decide to wrap up our training session, and Kiran offers to walk us both home. They both shiver in their winter clothes, but the outfit Cara made me is warm and comfortable, and with the protective spells Seath showed me, it is now quite weather resistant.

Seath breaks off on his own at the road with a short goodbye and a long look at Kiran that he ignores.

"I hope we can find the next thrall soon, it's always so cold up here," Kiran whines.

Cara chuckles. "I guess where you live it doesn't snow like this?"

He shakes his head, and I give him a pat on the shoulder. "Get used to it, it's only going to get colder from here."

"Historically the coming weeks mark a significant temperature drop. Using that data, I speculate that by next week we will start seeing lows of negative ten degrees celsius, or fourteen degrees fahrenheit," Celly explains.

Kiran shudders at the idea.

As we walk, we pass through a park at the end of the trail, with an old wooden playground and plenty of tall trees for kids to climb. A group of kids, all under the age of ten, crowd around one lone white cedar tree. When I look up, I notice a boy bravely climbing his way to the top.

I gesture to him and nudge Kiran. "Were you the type of kid to climb trees?"

"No," he says through chattered teeth. "I was the type to pretend a stick was a sword and run through the woods slaying dragons."

"I was the kid who wanted to play indoors all the time. Cara used to climb trees," I reply with a nostalgic smile creeping across my face.

"That's why this makes me nervous," she says, watching the boy intently. "You can fall way too easily, especially in this weather."

As if on cue, a snap reaches my ears and the boy freezes in terror for a moment, clinging to the trunk. He stays like that, breath held, for several seconds. He leans away from the tree and starts to relax, but as he slides his foot outward the branch gives way, and he falls.

I reach my hand out instinctively and draw a swirl of wind to catch the boy, gently floating him back down to the ground unharmed.

"What are you doing?" Kiran snaps. "If anyone sees you–"

"Was I supposed to let him fall? He could have broken his neck!" I reply.

"Nobody saw, so there's no harm done, anyways," Cara reasons, taking my arm and pulling me down the path.

We carry on walking, but I keep playing the interaction over in my head. Why is it that we have to hide our magic powers, anyways? What harm does it do? So what if people found out I could do magic? I tried to hide it from my parents, but only because I didn't know if they would believe me or understand why I wanted to learn.

The question presses in my mind, and even as I make it home, have dinner with my family, and get ready for bed, I can't quite figure out why it's seen as such a taboo.

"Celly?" I ask, sitting up in bed with the covers draped over my legs.

They levitate at eye level so I can see the enchanted avatar on screen clearly. "Yes?"

"Do you know why we are supposed to hide our magic powers?" I ask.

Without a moment's thought, they reply, "So that no one finds out."

136

"But why would it matter if people find out?"

They shrug. "I don't know, I only know what you tell me and what I can find on the internet, and data from online is woefully unreliable on this subject."

I suppose there is only one person who would know, but somehow I feel nervous about approaching Seath with this type of question. Maybe it's a silly thing to ask in the first place?

Still, just because I have to hide what I can do doesn't necessarily mean that I can't still use my power to help people. It felt good to help the boy today.

As I wake up in the morning earlier than usual, I go over the thoughts I had from the previous night. Early morning seems like a good time to test myself.

I wear a hooded jacket out and carry my grimoire under my arm and wander the neighborhood, but nothing really stands out to me. There's hardly anyone around, let alone anyone I can practice my powers on.

What can I do that would even help anyone anyways? I do have a healing spell that might be good at the hospital. But the hospital is at least 40 minutes away by bus.

As I wander aimlessly I find myself walking beyond the suburbs, where I spy an apartment building next to a church that is set apart from the stores around it—the apartments and church both have a lot of green space surrounding them, and they are both much nicer and cleaner than any other building around. As 7:00 am approaches, a handful of elderly folk in various states of mobility filter from the apartment to the church.

Perhaps common for early morning mass on a monday morning, not one attendee is younger than 60, which leaves me nervous as I approach the door. The only times I can remember being in a church have been for a couple of weddings.

It's a beautiful, wide building, with a steeple above the main entrance. The walls are painted white and the roof shingles are a simple gray. My hands shake a little as I grip the handles of the smoke-colored double-doors and pull one open.

The entryway is a small room with doors on every wall, including another set of double doors propped open just ahead, with a guestbook and a corkboard covered in various notices to its immediate left. I step through softly, keeping myself to the black carpet that lines the central aisle in the main room until I can sneak off to the rear-most pew.

In the main hall, four equal sets of oak pews are arranged in a large semi-circle around the elevated altar. I watch as a dozen seniors slowly take their seats among the first two rows. Two in particular seem to struggle immensely. I can see one man, thin and frail, wince and groan as he lowers himself onto the pew. Another is pushed in her wheelchair by a nurse, who parks her just at the foot of the altar off to the right. Each breath she takes seems like an agonizing wheeze.

I take my grimoire and flip through the pages. The healing spell would likely not be powerful enough to help anyone here—the help they need is much more intricate than my magic is capable of. In any case, that spell is more for physical injuries. But there is a spell that Seath had us copy that might be something—a spell to alleviate pain. Surely pain relief would be helpful to the people here.

138

The circle is elaborate in nature, with a flowery six-petal design. As I touch it, the circle glows a pale red along with my sigil. When I look up I can sense the pain each person is experiencing. Several have painful, aching hands, hips, and knees, most have back pain varying in severity, the wheelchair-bound woman has pain in her chest and joints, and the man who carries the most restrictive pain of all is the one who struggled to sit.

I focus on him first, keeping my left hand firmly planted on the magic circle. It takes a few moments, but as I feel the pain I sensed start to fade, I see him sit up straighter, rub his neck and inspect his hands in confusion. He suddenly seems much lighter, even younger-looking.

I repeat the process for every senior in there as the priest goes through the mass. It's tiring, and by the time I finish I feel so drained that I can barely bring myself to stand and sneak out the back. Though the walk to school from there is agonizing, I wear a smile through the exhausting trek.

XVIII.

Epidemic

The young boy sits at the edge of the playground, clutching a scraped knee. As I walked by, the boy and his friends had been running around the playground in spite of the ice and snow, throwing snowballs at each other. But this boy, no older than eight, slipped on the ice, and tore his pants at the knee, leaving a shallow but painful scrape across his bare skin.

I rush over and kneel beside him as tears well in his eyes, and the other children surround us with concern.

"Does it hurt?" I ask him as I open my grimoire. He nods. "Sit still a moment, I'll fix it."

I use the healing circle, and the kids stare wide-eyed as the circle glows for a moment and the skinned knee fades away until no trace of the injury remains.

"How did you do that?" the boy asks, wide-eyed.

I look around for a moment, then I whisper, "Can you keep a secret?"

The kids nod along, and I tell them, "I'm a witch."

"Like Harry Potter?" one kid asks. Another slaps his arms and mutters, "That's just a movie!"

I stand up and tuck my grimoire back into my bag with a smile. "Something like that."

As I walk away from the playground, I pass by a couple walking their dog. As they leave my field of view I hear both the man and woman cough rather violently, and I wonder for a moment if I can use my healing spell on them—but it would likely be unhelpful for healing illness.

The next day, as I arrive at school and find Cara waiting, I can't help but notice that the crowds are much thinner than usual. It's also much more quiet than other mornings—aside from the occasional cough, there is very little ambient noise filling the air.

"Hey!" Cara waves, with her usual big smile.

"How was your . . . club stuff yesterday?" I ask as I get close.

She laughs. "You don't even know what club I was at yesterday, do you?"

"You're in so many! I'm sorry, I can barely remember my own schedule." Though I feel like that's a fair excuse, a part of me still feels a pang of guilt—maybe because I know Cara wouldn't forget. I can't let my poor memory excuse being a sub-par friend to her when she is so reliably good to me.

"It was the school paper. Mr. Phillips talked to us about how big city newspapers find things to report on. He talked about how good journalists keep their eyes and ears open and pay attention to the community," she explains. "Speaking of being a good journalist, have you noticed how everyone seems sick today?"

Before I can answer, I spot Kiran approaching and wave him over and we exchange greetings.

"I have another circle I want to show you," he says as we start walking to our lockers. "It's a lightning spell, I think it would be good for you to have."

I nod and we make plans to go to the clearing again after school, then we head off to class. It doesn't occur to me until gym class when we barely have enough players to make two teams for ball hockey that over a third of my classmates are missing, and many of those who are here today seem to have a cough.

After school, as I pack up my bag at my locker, Kiran approaches, leaning against the neighboring locker door.

"Cara has club activities again today?" he asks.

I nod. "It's her gaming club today. Tomorrow she has Anime club in the morning, and book club after school."

"And what about you?"

I shrug. "I was in the book club, but I quit when Seath started teaching us magic."

"Then where have you been lately?" he asks, his eyes narrowed and his brow furrowed slightly, as if he is studying my face for an answer my words won't reveal.

"I don't know what you mean," I say sheepishly, trying to avoid his eyes. "I've been around."

142

"You disappeared after school yesterday, and the day before that you were almost late in the morning and then you disappeared again right when school ended," he says.

I haven't given Kiran enough credit, it would seem. He's been detail-oriented since we met, I should have realized he'd notice me acting weird. "I'm sorry, I guess I've been having an off week."

He holds his hand up to my forehead, waiting for me to give a slight nod of approval before he makes contact. "Hm, you're not warm, you don't have a fever. Maybe you're getting sick. I don't know if you've noticed, but it seems like there's a flu bug going around."

I close my locker and sling my backpack over my shoulder. "Honestly, I'm surprised I don't have it. I get sick pretty often."

"Magical people have better resistances to illness than most," he says dismissively. "Even if you do get sick, I'm sure Seath knows magic circles for helping with symptoms."

"Is there a cough suppressant spell?" I ask with a tinge of sarcasm.

"There's a spell for just about anything, really," he replies.

We make our way to the clearing in the woods from before, so that he can teach me new spells. He shows me a magic circle featuring a compass-like design and the centerpiece is a depiction of an orb with lightning-bolt designs coming off of it. With it I can create and control lightning—though despite my best efforts, so far the only thing I can create is a small spark that disappears in mere seconds.

Kiran's lightning—created with his sigil—is much more dramatic than mine. He makes it dance around him and controls it with precise motions.

"Has Seath taught you to multi-cast or project-cast yet?" Kiran asks as his lightning disperses.

I shake my head. "I don't even know what that means."

"As simply as possible," he says, "projection casting allows you to cast spells from your grimoire when its away from your person—in other words, you project the circle and activate it from a distance. As for a multi-cast, well that's just casting multiple spells at once."

"Do I need a circle to project-cast?"

He shakes his head. "The circle is already in your grimoire. As long as you have control over it and you can connect to the circle with your mind, you can project-cast on command."

I try it first with my grimoire open to the fire spell page. I concentrate on a fallen stick standing upright in the snow, and I focus on it until my head starts to hurt, but still nothing happens. I try to visualize the circle appearing until its image is seared into my eyes. I raise my hand, trying to mentally direct my energy in some way, and I stare until the image is so clear that I can see every minute detail even when I blink.

Finally, a small flame successfully ignites on the tip of the stick, no bigger than the flame of a candle. In a moment it is extinguished by the wind. I can feel my cheeks burning up from smiling so much, and Kiran pumps his arms up to the sky and shouts, "Yes!"

"I did it!" I yell out to the sky.

"And now that you can do that, you'll be able to eventually multi-cast in the same way."

We continue to practice together, and over several hours I am able to reignite my flame from a distance many more times.

As the sun sets, we gather our things and Kiran walks me home. Along the way, we notice a car pulling into the driveway of a house a little way up the street from us. A man gets out and has a severe coughing fit before finally composing himself and walking into his house.

"Wow," I say, as we walk by. "There really is something nasty going around."

I realize after a moment that Kiran has stopped. I look back, and he's looking all around the neighborhood with a scowl on his face.

"Kiran? What's wrong?"

"How did I not see this?" he spits out. "This is no ordinary sickness."

I pause and close my eyes for a moment and focus on my senses. It's faint, but I detect something, almost like a fog surrounding us. I open my eyes and can feel my heart racing. "This is magic?"

"Yes, it's a powerful miasma," Kiran says. "This is what's making everyone sick."

"Where is it coming from?" I ask, and he turns to me and immediately his eyes lock on something behind me. His face is dead serious.

"I have a pretty good guess," he mutters.

I turn around and come face to face with a large spectral skunk that has just leapt into the street, as large as a bear. From its tail I sense an invisible cloud of poison pouring into the air.

Of all the animals Yukiko could have chosen, she had to pick this one.

IXX.

Miasma

The tail of the skunk immediately sprays a thick, damp, olive-colored cloud in our direction. On reflex, I jump out of the way, scraping my elbow and tearing my coat on the icy layer over the curb.

Kiran puts up a transparent light barrier to intercept, but upon impact the cloud simply fans out. As it reaches him he throws his arm over his face and casts the physical enhancement spell so he can jump far back. As he lands, he starts coughing until he vomits a reddish bile.

"Don't let it touch you!" he calls, voice hoarse. "It's poisonous!"

I drag myself to my feet and run. Only after I have put plenty of distance between myself and the cloud do I stop to look around, realizing our opponent has run away.

Kiran rushes to my side. "We can't let her get away. If we don't stop her, the sick people are only going to get worse! Come on!"

I cast the enhancement spell on myself and immediately feel a surge of energy. I then use the magic tracing circle to detect the direction the skunk has gone. "She ran over the houses across the street, she's going from rooftop to rooftop!"

"Let's go!" Kiran says through another cough. His face seems much paler than before.

Together, we use the magic imbuing our bodies to effortlessly leap to the rooftops, then running from house to house and maintaining our balance as we follow our prey. The skunk is already quite far ahead, and evidently, she is far more nimble than us even with the magical enhancements we have, so despite our best efforts we lose sight of her. I scowl. We can't lose this chance.

After what feels like minutes of running, the tracing spell leads us off of the rooftops and back into the streets.

Kiran starts to lag behind as we come up on a more urban part of the town with shops and fewer houses. My senses tell me that the skunk crossed the street and followed the train tracks I can see between two buildings. As I approach the crosswalk, I hear Kiran wheezing, and I turn around to find him leaning against a lamppost, sickly and pale.

"Are you okay?" I ask, approaching him.

"I breathed in a concentrated dose of her miasma, so I'm really feeling it. But we can't . . . stop now," he says weakly, his voice raspy and off, as if he were speaking with his nose pinched. "Stopping her is the only way to cure everyone."

"You can't go on like this, you're about to pass out," I urge, placing a hand on his shoulder. "Look, I'm going to keep pursuing, so . . . call Cara and Seath, then go home."

"I'm fine, I can keep going–"

"You're not fine," I interrupt. I glance over my shoulder. "Look, we're going to lose her. This way I can keep following her."

"How will the others find you?"

I take Celly from my pocket and put them in Kiran's hand. "They can find me!"

Before he can protest, I take off across the street, down the alley, and along the train tracks. I follow the tracks until I am outside of the town limits. This is good, I won't have to worry about anyone else out here. I pass some trees and find an overgrown concrete field—and on the far end, near the rusted chain link fence, is the skunk.

I can't have her run again. I need to stop her, and a small kiddy flame won't cut it. People are counting on me.

As I walk closer, I use my grimoire to create a large wall of fire behind the skunk, causing her to jump closer to me.

The toll of using so many spells is already starting to bear down on me. I feel like I'm running low on energy.

Her tail arcs up over her back and aims right at me. Judging from what happened to Kiran, I can't risk blocking the shot. I have to dodge. As the olive spray comes right at me, I jump to the side and try out the new lightning spell. My grimoire flips open to the page and the circle appears at my fingertips, and sparks and small arcs start to generate in my hand and between my fingers. A bolt shoots out, just barely missing her as she dodges away.

As she turns to run, I spark up another fire wall behind her at the fence line.

She begins firing shot after shot in my direction, forcing me to repeatedly dodge. Somehow it seems easy—as if her aim is off. As a shot fires off far to my left, I realize why.

She's not aiming for me.

Everywhere her shots landed has formed a thick, poisonous fog, and I am now surrounded. My only option for escape is to charge directly at her, and she is poised to intercept me.

Still, it's either try or let the miasma take me. I cast the blade of lightning Kiran taught me and project-cast the lightning bolt spell to try and hit her from above as I run forward.

As I do, she avoids the lightning bolt and fires at me. Still imbued with the enhancement magic, I instinctively leap over the poisonous fog, but as I do she fires right into my path.

I have no means of changing my trajectory or blocking the shot.

I instinctively throw my sigil hand in front of myself, and as if responding to my fear, it begins to glow. In that instance, a great storm of wind hits the whole field, forcing the shot off course and sweeping all of the poisonous fog away at once, and exerting intense pressure on the skunk spirit. With her trapped by the winds, I swing the lightning blade out, and an arc flies off from the blade into her, shocking her until she collapses. As I land I dismiss the blade and the wind stops.

Her eyes meet mine as I kneel down right in front of her and reach out my hand, gently brushing her spectral fur.

"I know you're scared and you're looking for Yukiko," I say softly. "She isn't here anymore, I'm sorry. Please, let me take away your fear. It's alright."

As her eyes close, she turns into a stone like the others, gently forming in the palm of my hand.

As my heart rate begins to return to normal and the adrenaline wears off, the exhaustion begins to take over. I stumble trying to stand, and my eyelids feel incredibly heavy. My second attempt causes me to collapse and drift into unconsciousness.

When I wake up, I find myself back in bed at home. I feel something clutching my hand, and groggily I start to sit up, only for my eyes to be assailed by a bright light.

"She's up! Cara, she's awake!" I hear Celly's voice say as my eyes adjust to their bright screen and I make out the giddy face of their avatar.

I look over to see Cara clutching my hand, asleep with her knees to her chest in a chair pulled to my bedside. She rubs her eyes as she stirs, and her lips curl into a big smile once she gains awareness.

"Thank goodness you're okay," she says. "Seath and Celly found you passed out. He said you just over-exerted yourself but . . ."

"Cara never left your side," Celly interrupts. "She was worried for you."

"I'm sorry I didn't reach out," I say. "Everything happened so fast and–"

"I know," Cara says. "Kiran told us everything."

"Is Kiran okay?" I ask, glancing around the room for him. "What about everyone else who was sick?"

Celly nods through their avatar. "As the magical source of the illness was subdued, the spell was broken and everyone who was sick recovered within six hours. Kiran included."

"Kiran's mom came to get him," Cara adds. "And don't worry, Seath is explaining everything to your parents downstairs."

"So," I say, looking out the window into the dark. "Only two spirits are left to capture."

I wonder what comes next once I've finished finding all the thralls? Did Yukiko see this far into the future? Did she have some sort of plan for me?

In the distance, despite the dark, I can make out a pair of eagle eyes. The bird sits perched on a powerline, and after a moment, it flies away.

XX.

The Limits of Magic

Rumors are a funny thing. As I walk to school on this chilly morning, I scroll through the blog that Cara texted me. It's a story about a miracle worker in the city. Despite the overt religious inferences of the writer, it's obvious the story is about me—it describes in clear detail some of the things I've done with my magic, like easing the pain of the elderly and disabled throughout the town, or tending to kids who have gotten bumps and scrapes. There are other stories that are unfamiliar to me as well, though. It seems like almost every random act of good luck is being attributed to this mysterious healer.

It's amusing to read what people think—the author and several commenters clearly think there is some sort of holy miracle at work, while others are skeptical and attribute everything to chance and showmanship. It makes me feel like a secret superhero, though the threats I deal with are hardly world-changing.

"Hey, Celly," I ask, causing their avatar to take over the screen. "There must be other witches out there other than me, right?"

"To my knowledge, you are the heir of the Witch of the Full Moon, a woman named Elatha Yukiko. I can't find anything about her on the internet, though," they reply. "Other than you, the only other witch I know of is Cyra Oralie, the Witch of the Sun. There is a woman with that name who lives in Florida. She is apparently a known philanthropist, but I've seen no evidence of her magical activities."

"Kiran is Cyra's vassal, I wonder if he knows any other witches?"

"I wouldn't know," Celly replies. "Maybe you should talk to him about it!"

It does seem strange to me. Yukiko was clearly much more powerful than I am, and Cyra sounds very powerful, too. What are they doing with their magic? How are they not famous? Are they hiding on purpose?

A yawn escapes my lips as I approach the school. Ever since last week's fight against the skunk thrall, I've felt so tired all the time. It's like I have no energy. I don't know what's wrong with me.

Kiran and Cara are both waiting for me at the school's entrance. I haven't seen Kiran since the last battle, but thankfully he looks well—for the most part. He stands bundled in a burly black winter coat and a thick wool scarf, with his gloved hands tucked under his arms.

"Cold?" I ask him with a little grin.

"I hate this frozen wasteland," he barks back behind chattering teeth.

"It's only going to get colder," Cara says as we begin walking toward the building. "Today it's supposed to start snowing."

Sure enough, by lunch time the snow has started falling, leaving a pretty dusting over everything. Throughout the day, I keep finding myself staring off into the distance, watching the flakes fall lazily from the gray sky. It's soothing, and leaves me feeling sleepy.

After school, I meet with Kiran at the school entrance once more, so we can walk to our training spot while Cara has her club activities.

"What are we going to practice today?" I ask him as we walk.

He shrugs. "I thought we could take it easy today."

"I'm sorry, are you not recovered yet?" I ask, concern flitting through me. "That last battle was rough."

"It's not me," he says, a concerned look in his eyes. "It's you, Selena. You need a break. You're pushing your limits, so I thought we could go to Seath's home and see if he can do anything to help."

It's true that I've been feeling tired all of the time, and even during the last battle I felt like I was running on fumes from the beginning. It's only gotten worse since then. No matter how much I sleep, I'm still tired.

"Do you think something's wrong with me? Maybe it's from one of the spirits?" I ask, a growing sense of anxiety in my chest.

Kiran shakes his head. "I don't think it's anything that dramatic. You've just been using a lot of magic and you've stretched yourself thin. You're still learning, and you'll get stronger the more you develop your powers, but for now you need a break."

"Is it the same for you?"

He looks up at the clouds. "Yes. It took a lot of discipline to develop my stamina. I've been training under my Mistress for four years. I've got to say, Cyra is a much stricter teacher than Seath. But of course, it's different for her. Seath wants to train you to be independent, but for Cyra she's training us to be soldiers. It's considered an honor to be one of her vassals. It's very competitive."

"Does she have a lot of them?" I ask, curious. I wonder if I will have vassals one day, or even a consort. If I were to share my power with anyone, it would probably be Cara.

"She has five. Five is kind of a special number for her, some witches have affinities for stuff like that. I'm the youngest, of course, so it's tough. This is my first mission, and it's my only chance to prove to Cyra that I deserve my position. The others already earned their place, so they kind of look down on me."

I want to ask more, but we are already at Seath's house. He is standing on the porch, a mug in his hand, as if he's been expecting us. With his long gray overcoat over his black turtleneck and ashy jeans, he looks somewhat regal—perhaps fittingly, as former consort to the Witch of the Full Moon.

He has a serious look on his face, and he is staring off into space as if looking past us. When I look over my shoulder I catch a glimpse of a bird—perhaps an eagle— flying off.

"Do you have any more of that?" Kiran asks as we get close.

Seath smirks. "*This* has liquor in it, so no. Come inside and get warm, I'll fix you something a little more appropriate."

Seath lets us in and leads us to sit around the fire as he prepares two mugs of cocoa for Kiran and I. He hands them off to us as he leaves the kitchen and stands by the fire, leaning one of his arms on the mantle.

It's quiet, and there is an uncomfortable tension in the air. I look between Kiran and Seath, wondering if they also feel this sense of awkwardness, but their expressions give nothing away. I suppose Seath and Kiran still have some trust issues between them, perhaps that's it? Once I finish my drink and put it down, Seath clears his throat and looks at me.

"Do you know you have rings under your eyes?" he asks. "Have you been having trouble sleeping lately?"

I touch my face instinctively, feeling self conscious. "It's more like I've been having trouble waking up."

"And no matter how much you sleep, it never feels like it's enough?" he presses, and I nod in reply. "It's because your magical powers are strained. You're pushing your limits and over-using your powers."

"But I don't feel like I really used that much power when I fought against the skunk spirit," I say. "It took a lot to beat her, but I used a lot of power against the other thralls, too."

"That's not what's draining you. It certainly didn't help, but It's all your active spells that you have out there."

"I can sense it all over town," Kiran adds. "Traces of your magic."

"I don't understand," I say, looking between him and Kiran.

"You've been using magic recklessly," Seath says. "You've drawn attention to yourself, and because of that I was able to figure out what you were doing. We're going to talk about that, because that's an important problem too, but right now this is about you using your power to try and heal everyone you come across. That's what you've been doing, right?"

I nod solemnly. "I thought since I had this power I could use it to help people."

"Every time you've used magic like that, you've created an active spell, and each active spell you have drains your power bit by bit," Seath says. "Over a short amount of time, it's not that bad. But as you can see, the more you do it, the more it drains your power—and the more it drains you, the more it affects you physically.

"And it's not just you," Seath presses. "When you get so exhausted that you can't keep your eyes open, your power wanes and everyone influenced by your magic feels it. And when you go after a thrall, you're forced to push yourself to your absolute limit. That puts you and your friends in danger. You need to release all of these spells, so you can recover properly."

But thinking it over, I dread the very idea. "What will happen to all those people if I do that?"

"The spell's effects will wear off," Kiran answers.

"Then I can't," I argue. "I'm helping them. If the effects wear off, they're going to be in pain again."

"You have to," Seath says, walking over to me. "You aren't going to get better. Your powers are going to be continually drained until it starts to affect your health, and then you can get seriously ill, maybe even die."

He kneels in front of me and takes my hands in his. "I know you want to help people, but this doesn't help them. Magic can't solve every problem. There is a reason Yukiko didn't go around trying to heal everyone. Say one of the people you helped needs nursing care. You take away his pain, and that lasts for a few weeks, or as long as you can hold out. If he loses his nursing care because he seems to be better, then once your spell wears off he will be in serious trouble. It is not a kindness to make people depend on your magic."

Tears start to well in my eyes. "I just wanted to help."

He gently brushes a tear from my cheek. His hand warms my face and reminds me a bit of dad. "You will help many people with your power, and the stronger you get the more people you can help. But you can't help anyone if you're too drained to do anything, Selena. Let go, let yourself recover. And when you're back to 100 percent, I'll teach you some things you can do with your magic to really help the community."

When I close my eyes and concentrate, I can feel my magical presence being pulled in dozens of different directions. I focus and envision it as a series of chains around my aura, siphoning it. And in my imagination, I feel the chains break, one by one, until I am completely liberated.

I feel an immediate rush of energy, my lethargy disappearing. It's a bittersweet feeling—on one hand I finally feel like myself again, but on the other, I can't stop thinking about all the people who will suddenly find their pain returning.

I have to do better in the future. I can't make another mistake like this.

XXI.

Kinship

I thought that once my exhaustion was gone, my anxiety would also dissipate, but now that I am finally alert again, I can't shake the feeling that I'm being watched. Throughout the morning, every time I find myself in view of a window, I get the eerie sense that something is watching me, but whenever I look, nothing is there.

Not only that, but I keep having dreams in which I'm standing in the schoolyard. It is a beautiful moonlit night, and everything is peaceful, but then the sun rises and completely erases the moon from the sky, and when I turn to look at the sun I become petrified with fear.

Perhaps the real reason for my anxiety, though, has something to do with my plans for today. I inspect my outfit in the mirror—an oversized black and white striped sweater and black leggings—and hope that it is good for a first impression. I send a photo to Cara looking for her affirmation, and she quickly texts back that I look good.

I've been nervous ever since Kiran invited Cara and I over to meet his parents yesterday. I wonder what they are like. Kiran seems like a serious person, so his parents are likely serious people, too. The thought is intimidating, and it dominates my attention so much that I jump a little when the doorbell rings.

I grab my backpack with my grimoire inside and rush down to the front door, where Cara is waiting, dressed nicely in a dark green sweater over a plaid button-up shirt and pale-blue jeans.

"Ready?" she asks with a smile. She has clearly done her makeup—she looks beautiful in a mature, feminine way.

I nod, feeling a little self-conscious compared to her glamor.

We walk across town toward Kiran's home. He lives a bit further north of my house, across from a little strip mall with a grocery store, a pharmacy, and ten different small food places—I know the area pretty well, having gone to that strip many times with Mom and Dad.

The entire walk I keep getting that same uncomfortable sense of being watched. At one point, from the corner of my eyes, I spy a large eagle in the distance, but it is already taking off by the time I notice, and when I try to get a better look it ducks behind some distant buildings.

We come up to three identical five-story brown apartment buildings surrounding a pretty little greenspace filled with empty flower beds. Cara and I stop at the driveway, and I look between the three buildings.

"Which one is it?" I ask.

Cara smiles, her eyes locked on the middle building. "It's that one."

As I follow her gaze, I see Kiran waving from the far balcony in the middle building on the top floor. He's bundled up, and I swear I can feel him shivering even from this distance. Was he waiting for us the whole time in the cold?

He disappears into the apartment, so Cara and I approach the front entrance. We reach the doors just in time for Kiran to walk out of the elevator and open them for us.

His cool gray flannel shirt seems brand new. I wonder if he bought it just for today.

He escorts Cara and I across the lobby, past the rental office on the right and mail room on the left, to the elevators on the far wall, which then takes us up to the top floor. His apartment sits in the corner, down the brown-carpeted hallway.

"Take your shoes off inside, please," he instructs as he opens the door to his apartment.

It's a beautiful space, with white walls and grey-and-black furniture. A long, ash-colored couch, flanked by armchairs on either side, sits opposite a large wall-mounted TV, and in the corner past the TV is a desk with a computer. And, of course, the entrance to the balcony in the opposite corner. Kiran takes our coats as we get our shoes off and hangs them up in the living room closet.

I take another look around, peering down the long hall to the left. To my right is the kitchen entrance, which uses thin gray curtains for a door. There is a large painting above the couch of a beautiful countryside,

164

and all the other walls are adorned with various family photos.

All of the sudden, I hear a sound like rapid tapping, and a big fluffy dog with thick curly gold fur and a big goofy expression comes running out from one of the bedrooms, wagging her tail.

"Sovanna, sit," Kiran commands.

The dog skids to a halt along the hardwood floors and sits, barely containing her jittery excitement.

"I remember you said you have a dog!" Cara squeals. "Can we pet her?"

"Yeah, she's friendly, go ahead."

Cara and I both reach for the dog and run our hands against her soft wooly fur as she excitedly sniffs us and licks our hands and presses herself against our legs.

Finally Kiran claps his hands to get her attention and commands her to "go lie down," causing the dog to happily trot off to a giant gray pillow on the ground tucked beside the balcony door.

At that moment, a man and woman emerge from the kitchen. The man is relatively short—almost equal to my height—and has a full face, with round cheeks and messy dark curls. The woman, on the other hand, is nearly as tall as Seath and full-figured, with long, reddish-black wavy hair and rectangular glasses. Evidently, Kiran has his father's coloring, but his mother's face and height.

"Hello, ladies," Mr. Hoku says with a smile. "Please make yourselves at home. Dinner will be ready in just a bit."

Mrs. Hoku has a kind expression, but the way she gazes at me makes me feel small—as if she's studying me thoroughly, trying to figure me out. "Kiran," she says in a soothing tone. "Why don't you give your friends a tour?"

Kiran and Cara step toward the hall, and I turn to join them, but I freeze in place as I feel Mrs. Hoku's hand clasp my shoulder. I look back at her, and she remains still until Kiran and Cara have disappeared into the far bedroom. Instead, Mrs. Hoku leads me over to the window, where she looks out into the distance.

"I sense the power of the moon in you," she says finally. "You remind me a lot of your predecessor. You have her face."

I'm not sure what to say. I open my mouth to speak, but nothing comes out. I don't know how much she knows about magic or anything else, after all. I don't want to say something that puts Kiran in a precarious position.

"I saw Yukiko once, when I was just a little girl. I remember thinking she was the most elegant thing I had ever seen in all my life. She was a beautiful woman, but very troubled." She pauses, then turns to face me. "Has that man, Seath, ever told you about your predecessor?"

I shake my head. "He hasn't said much. I think talking about her makes him sad."

"No one in this world loved Yukiko more than Seath Faolan, except maybe Cyra Oralie."

I blink. Cyra loved Yukiko? But that goes against everything I've heard. "Everyone told me they were enemies."

Mrs. Hoku smiles. "A long time ago they were close, but they had a fight. The collapsing of their relationship hurt Cyra deeply. For a long time they have been enemies, and even in death, Yukiko's magic works to undermine Cyra's purposes. Yet, despite their conflict, you, Heir to the Moon, and Kiran, Vassal of the Sun, have met and become friends. There must be some meaning in that. Perhaps your friendship is a sign that things are changing, finally. But that all depends on Cyra. Just know," she says, looking deep into my eyes, "I am rooting for your generation."

Before I can reply, Kiran returns, eyeing us suspiciously. I suppose his mom never told him she planned to talk to me.

Mr. Hoku calls us in for dinner, and the rest of the evening is spent casually socializing, but I can't get what Mrs. Hoku said out of my head. I keep replaying it all in my mind. It weighs on me even as we finally get ready to leave after dinner.

As Kiran walks us home, I start to wonder what Mrs. Hoku meant when she said that it *all depends on Cyra.* I look up to the sky and catch a glimpse of an eagle soaring in the distance.

For a split second, I could swear it was watching me, but it could just be my imagination.

XXII.

The Earth and the Sky

"Remind me why we're out here?" Cara says as we walk through a park trail, leaving imprints on the fresh snow along the path. She carries her bow and quiver in a case over her shoulder.

"Ask him," I say as I use my magic detection spell to no avail, Celly levitating at shoulder height around me.

Kiran tucks his arms in, shivering. "We can't just wait for the last of Yukiko's thralls to show up. That's how we ended up getting blindsided by the skunk and letting half the town get sick. We should start being more proactive. Selena's senses have gotten strong enough that If we patrol the town, we should eventually come across some trace of them."

"What if they left town?" Cara asks. "The last two are an owl spirit and the wolf that attacked Selena and I, right? They could be halfway across the country by now."

"They wouldn't leave on their own accord," Kiran says. "They are ultimately freaking out because they are

168

bound to Yukiko and she's not here. But they can still detect the presence of the moon because of the old house—and Selena, of course. It's like being told something is there, yet they can't find it."

"I can't sense anything," I finally say, cutting off the spell.

Kiran is undeterred by our repeated failings despite my own disheartened reaction, though, so we press on as a group, continuing our search. Every so often I'll activate the detection spell and use it to scan an area, but after several hours out we still come up with nothing.

It's dark out, despite being only five o'clock. It feels like midnight.

Kiran decides to take a break—he can tell everyone is hungry. So together, we stop for pizza and pop at a little place with only two tables and six chairs. I text mom and dad to let them know I won't need dinner, and place Celly face up on the table so they can listen while we talk.

"So what happens after we catch the last two thralls?" Cara asks.

Kiran shrugs. "I'll go back to Florida to report to Mistress Cyra, and continue my training as her Vassal. There's not much else for me to do, up here."

His words sting. "I guess I hadn't thought of that," I mutter, staring into the black abyss that is my soda.

"We'll probably continue training under Seath," Cara says. "I can't imagine going to school without you, though, that's going to be weird. You'll have to keep in touch! Maybe during summer break we'll come down and visit, if that's okay."

"Well, sure, our house in Florida has lots of space, plus there's Cyra's estate. I'm sure you'd be welcome down there," he replies, looking over at me. "I know her and Seath have their issues, but Cyra really isn't so bad as long as you respect her rules."

"We can apply for jobs after we finish getting the thralls. Do you want to do that?" Cara asks, her eyes on me.

A smile creeps across my face. "I'd like that. And, hey, by summer I'll probably know some more stuff and I could even teach you some things!"

"I can estimate the cost of this trip for you," Celly pipes up. "So that you know how much money you need to have saved."

"Thank you, Celly," Cara says with a grin.

After eating, we decide to do another round of patrolling, just to be safe. Even if we don't find anything, it's fun exploring the city with my friends. It really will be hard once Kiran goes home, but Cara's optimism does make me feel better. I guess there are a lot of ways to keep in touch online while we're apart, and if we work and save our money, we could definitely go down to Florida for summer break.

Eventually, our path takes us to the woods near Yukiko's manor. It's quiet, and yet something makes me anxious. I can't tell exactly what it is, but on instinct, I take my grimoire out and cast my detection spell.

"Kiran! Cara!" I call. "I feel something in the distance!"

Sure enough, I can see something—a spectral owl, massive in size, her wings spread wide. She looks at us from afar and veers towards the woods.

"Follow her!" Kiran shouts, taking off into the woods.

Cara waves me on ahead as she takes a moment to retrieve her bow and quiver, so I take off after Kiran. As I run, I cast a trail of fairy lights for Cara to follow. It's dark, and I can't see the sky through the trees, so I rely entirely on my magical senses to guide me.

My senses lead me to a large clearing, where Kiran is waiting. The owl spirit sits perched atop a tree on the far side. I raise my hand and use my sigil to cast dozens of fairy lights all around so that we can see.

Kiran scowls. "She's coming!"

Just as he speaks, the owl clings to the tree and beats her wings violently, creating powerful blasts of wind strong enough to knock us both down. Kiran fires a bolt of fire at her, but she soars from her perch and divebombs him. He narrowly rolls out of the path of her talons, and I watch in horror as they tear up the frozen earth where he once was with ease. If her talons are that powerful, then we cannot allow her to grab us.

I remote cast lightning strikes from above to try to catch her, but she flies high into the sky and dodges my every attack. She circles around and comes barrelling toward me at blinding speed.

Before I can even react, she is in my face with her talons poised, but in the moment before she grabs me a flaming arrow flies between us, and she aborts her attack at the last second to avoid being hit.

I look from the direction of the shot and see Cara emerge from the woods, bow in hand.

"She's fast," Celly chimes, flying up from my pocket. "Our best strategy would be to try and restrict her movements so that Cara can land a direct hit."

Kiran creates a flame sword in his hand and begins firing several fireballs into the air around the owl.

I focus and use the lightning spell to send arcing bolts in her path. Between Kiran and I, we are able to narrow the owl's path, And with a screech that splits the air, she divebombs Kiran once again. Cara aims her bow, the spell she cast before igniting the tip of her arrow. I follow the Owl with more lightning so she cannot dodge the arrow like last time, and Kiran takes a stance with his sword.

Suddenly, I hear Cara scream, and her arrow shoots way off course. Kiran dodges, but the owl's talons graze his side, drawing blood. I turn to Cara to find the wolf spirit pinning her down, snarling in her face.

"Cara!" I shout, raising my hand instinctively, causing ice stalagmites to form and twist toward the wolf. She jumps free from Cara, landing across the clearing, as the owl circles above.

Both Cara and Kiran rise to their feet and come to either side of me.

"What do we do? We've never fought two at once before," Cara says.

Celly flies over to Kiran. "With your injuries, you might have to retire from this fight."

He shrugs them off. "I'm fine. We don't have a choice, this is it."

"I agree," I say finally, summoning a lightning blade to one hand and casting the physical enhancement spell to boost my strength and agility. "We can do this together!"

XXIII.

The Last Trial

Though we have managed to hold our own for some time, the battle is growing desperate. Every time we try to focus our attention on stopping the owl, the wolf spirit intervenes and stops us. Every time we try to fight off the wolf, the owl divebombs us. Together, they form a nigh-unstoppable force.

Though Kiran continues to act tough, I can tell his injury is starting to really weigh on him. He's starting to look faint. Though the cuts in his side are shallow, they have bled quite a bit and it must hurt a lot for him to move.

Cara is also running out of stamina—and arrows. I can see she only has four or five left in her quiver.

The wolf charges at me. Instinctively, I throw up a barrier spell, but the owl rushes me from behind. Kiran jumps to my back and slashes his flame sword, sending an arc of fire toward her, so she veers off course.

The wolf jumps around my barrier, but I create another wall of ice stalagmites to intercept her. Kiran uses the physical enhancement spell to jump over them and engage the wolf directly.

"Focus on the owl!" he shouts. "I'll hold this one off!"

"Celly," I call. "Use the barrier spell to protect his left side where he's hurt!"

Cara runs over to me as I use my sigil to manipulate the water in the air to form into ice darts to shoot toward the owl. At the same time, I summon lightning strikes from above to try and slow her movements. Without even having to ask, Cara takes aim and fires an arrow into the sky, but the owl has grown wise to our tactics and avoids it.

"We need to try something new," I call.

I try to think, but the owl perches on the treetop and knocks us all down with blasts of wind again, following it up with a divebomb. She soars toward Cara, and on instinct I rise to my feet and jump for her. I cover her with my body, and at that moment I feel an intense searing pain across my back as the talons close around me. I scream as she tears off into the sky with me in tow, and I can already feel streams of warm blood against my back where the talons have sunken in.

The owl flies me high into the air and drops me. I cast the feather-fall spell Kiran taught me just before I crash into the ground. My whole body aches, and every small movement causes pain to shoot from my wounds.

Cara rushes to my side as I watch the owl soaring in circles in the sky.

"Selena! Are you okay?" Cara says through tears, kneeling beside me to inspect my wounds.

I don't answer. Instead, I think back to the first spell I learned from Seath. I recall how the magical circle lit up and turned our subpar lawn into a perfect, lush patch of vibrant grass.

"Cara, on my mark I need you to shoot toward the tree, where the owl usually lands," I say. I look over at her and she nods meaningfully and draws another arrow, taking aim.

As the owl flies toward the tree, I remote cast that first magic circle, focusing on the tree. In the instant before the owl lands, the tree explodes into a full spring bloom, startling her.

Cara understands my tactic immediately. She fires at the moment the owl is stunned, and on impact, the arrow turns into a burst of fire, igniting her and causing her to glide toward the ground, crashing violently into the earth.

"Restrain her!" I say, so Cara leaves my side for the owl.

I fight through the pain and force myself to stand. When I look over to Kiran, I can see him growing more and more tired. The wolf slaps Celly away with her paw then jumps at Kiran, headbutting him in the stomach and knocking him back. As she approaches him, I cast a fireball to catch her attention.

She stalks toward me. Between the pain from my back and my general exhaustion, I don't have much fight left in me. On one side I can see Cara, standing by the restrained owl spirit. On the other side, I can see Kiran rising to his knees.

We're all exhausted and at our limits. I need to rely on my magical instincts. Forget everything else, and just feel the world around me. Feel the powers of the moon.

The wolf lunges and I throw my hand up in my face, and a wall of water materializes in her path. As she passes through the water, it disappears and a mirror copy of the wolf comes out the other end. The wolves land in tandem. They both look back at the same time, inspecting each other—the false wolf copying the real one's movements exactly. I'm not even sure what I did, and before I can take a moment to think about it, she ignores her doppelganger and jumps on me, pinning me to the ground.

Just as she opens her jaw to bite, I raise my hand to the false wolf, and I fully understand my spell in that instant. With a single thought, I make the fake stop, and in doing so the real wolf becomes frozen.

I can control the doppelganger.

"Attack the fake!" I shout, and Cara fires her last arrow while Kiran fires a bolt of lightning, both striking the false wolf at the same time. The doppelganger is destroyed, causing the real wolf to collapse, disabled.

I climb out from under her and struggle to my feet.

"Yukiko isn't here anymore. She passed away a long time ago. I know that you're scared, but you're not alone. I promise, I will help you," I say softly to them both. The owl relents, turning into her small stone form and coming to my palm, but the wolf continues to resist.

Though she has no energy left to fight, she snarls and barks at me. I gently place my hand on her head and pet her.

Through our touch, I can sense her thoughts.

I'll never leave you, a distant voice echoes in my mind. The wolf calms, and when she looks into my eyes I can suddenly see a memory.

> *Yukiko sits at the edge of the lake, her thralls surrounding her.*
>
> *"I won't be here much longer, my dears," she says as a lime-green moth hovers into her outstretched palm. "I'll be putting you all to sleep for a time. But when you wake up, come and find me."*
>
> *The wolf whines and rubs her muzzle against Yukiko's chest. She smiles slightly, and pets the spectral beast. "Don't be scared. I'll never leave you. Not really. Everything is going to happen just the way it was always meant to."*

As the memory fades, the wolf's eyes close and she submits, returning to her stone form as well.

With the battle over, the exhaustion quickly takes over, and I collapse in the clearing.

XIV.

A True Witch

I find myself wandering alone in the woods in the early morning, compelled by some force—or perhaps dream logic. The rising sun shines brightly enough that I have to cover my eyes to protect them as I leave the woods. Blinking against it, I can just mark the area as the track field from school.

In the distance, I can see a collapsed figure in the middle.

As I approach, I realize that it is an old gray wolf, with the eagle I keep dreaming about perched menacingly atop his withered form. The wolf seems to be injured, and I want to help him, but the eagle scares me. She watches my every step, and when I get close she squawks and flares her wings aggressively. I try to reach out to the wolf, but the eagle bites me.

The shock jolts me awake, and I shoot up in bed.

"Are you okay, Selena?" Celly asks, levitating in front of me.

I rub my eyes, still feeling groggy. "Just another dream. I keep dreaming about that eagle."

"You have mentioned this before. I believe you have also told me that you sometimes feel like you're being watched outside of your dreams, too."

I nod.

"Have you told Seath, Cara, or Kiran?" they ask.

I shake my head. "It's probably nothing."

I push the dream from my head. Today is a special day after all.

With the final spirit collected, Seath plans to throw us a little party at the manor. What, exactly, Seath considers a party I can't say, but he was surprisingly excitable when he invited me.

I dress up in the outfit Cara made for me, though I keep the cape and hat safely in my bag instead of wearing them out, deciding to wait until I have reached Seath's driveway to put them on.

I find him standing at the tree out front the house, just like the day we met. His hand is on the trunk, and he is looking off into the distance, as if seeing something I can not. There is the faintest smile on his face, and I can see his lips moving, but he is speaking too low for me to hear. As I get closer, he looks over at me.

"Am I the first one here?" I ask, stopping just in front of him.

He nods.

"You were talking to this tree back then, too, weren't you?"

He looks at me with surprise, too stunned to reply for a moment. "Back when?"

"When we first met here."

He looks away for a moment, lost in memory. "That's right, I was."

I reach my hand out and touch the tree. I can feel a familiar magical presence coming from within.

"I come out here sometimes to talk to her, though I'm not sure if she can hear me from wherever she is," he replies. "It helps clear my head."

How much of this happened as Yukiko planned, I wonder. I don't think even Seath knows how far she saw into the future, and what plans she laid out for me.

I look up and notice a green moth resting among the branches.

Seath puts his hand on my shoulder. "I'm proud of you. And I know Yukiko would be, too."

Before I can answer, I hear my name being called. I turn to see Kiran and Cara walking up the driveway.

Seath leads us all inside, where he's decorated the dining room with a colorful banner that reads "Congratulations, gang!". Taped to the ceiling are bits of thread with cartoony plastic moons and stars hanging on the end, and Seath brings out a tray of cupcakes and three mugs of hot cocoa. The cupcakes are decorated with swirls of frosting that go from deep midnight blue to snow-white at their tips, with silver sprinkles.

"These are beautiful!" I say, inspecting them. "Thank you so much!"

"Don't thank me," Seath replies. "I couldn't boil water. Kiran made them."

Kiran smiles. "It was nothing. Baking is a hobby of mine. My aunt owns a bakery, and she taught me how to use magic to help with it."

"I'd love to learn," Cara chimes in. "I can cook, but I've always wanted to learn how to make sweets!"

"I'll text the spells and recipes to you," he replies with an easy smile.

Seath disappears into the kitchen for a moment and comes out with a mug of his own, leaning against the doorframe.

"So, kid, I guess you'll be moving on soon, right?" Seath says.

Kiran nods, wiping a bit of frosting from the corner of his mouth and setting his cupcake down. "That's right. I'm going to stay for the holidays, but I'll be leaving the day after Christmas."

"What are you going to tell Cyra?" His expression is grave as he asks.

"Over the phone, I told her it was just an inexperienced witch who lost control of her thralls. I am still bound by our promise spell, so I will say nothing of Selena, Cara, or you, though I don't think you have to worry. I know you don't trust her, but she's a fair person. She'll understand. Selena isn't Yukiko. Whatever grudge they had against each other has been over since before Selena and I were even born."

"Have you met other witches?" Celly asks Kiran.

He nods. "Well sure, I've met a few others. Cyra works with other witches all the time."

"I'd love to meet others like me," I add. "I wonder if they can teach me other forms of magic?"

"I'm guessing you're pretty young for a witch," Cara says. "Most of them are adults, right?"

Seath nods.

After a short silence, more casual conversation resumes—topics besides witches and magic.

The party is fun. After eating way too many cupcakes, Seath brings out a board game where each of us controls a little army and competes for control. There is a lot of shouting throughout the game, but in the end Celly easily defeats all of us. After, Seath offers to teach us how to play different types of poker games.

I excuse myself from the table to stretch my legs, and I wander through the house, finding myself in the study. I look out the window, watching the lake for a moment, until footsteps catch my attention.

I turn to see Kiran standing in the doorway. He walks over and stands beside me, facing the window.

"Before I go home, I wanted to give you a little something. A Christmas gift, I guess," he says. He seems strangely awkward—usually he speaks so clearly and confidently.

He hands me a box, and I open it. Inside is a little silver crescent moon brooch. I take it out and hold it in my hands. "It's beautiful. Thank you so much, Kiran."

He blushes a little and his shoulders go up awkwardly, as if he's making himself smaller. "I saw it in a shop and thought of you. I got one for Cara, too, a little bow and arrow."

I give him a little hug, then I pin the brooch over my left breast, admiring how it looks in my reflection in the window.

"I have something for you, too," I say. "Come here!"

I lead him to the front foyer where I left my bag behind and fish inside, retrieving a box in Christmas wrapping paper, which I hand to him.

He chuckles and tears the paper apart, then opens the box inside, revealing a black leather bookbag.

"It's for your grimoire," I tell him.

He smiles and returns my hug from earlier. "It's perfect. Thank you, Selena."

I'm going to miss him a lot when he goes back to Florida.

XXV.
The Golden Eagle

It's the last day of school before winter break. It's a little warmer out this morning than it's been previously, which I consider a bit of a blessing on my walk, though the sun has melted all the snow and that makes me a little sad. I hope it snows again before Christmas.

I have my witch outfit and little else. I suppose not much else is needed for the last day. The last day of school before holidays is always traditionally a half-day, since there is almost never any schoolwork to assign that hasn't already been handed out the day prior.

As I approach the school, I can see the eagle from my dreams perched on top of the building. It watches me intently. My intuition tells me it's an ominous sign, but I won't let it distract me. Kiran is going home soon, and I want to enjoy the time I have left with him.

Cara and Kiran wait for me at the front entrance, like usual. I greet them and we head on inside to our lockers.

The school day is pretty casual. In first period, after wishing the teacher happy holidays, we are free to socialize, so Kiran, Cara, and I are able to sit around my desk and talk. It's liberating, in a way, to not have some pressing mission to focus on. Whenever we talked before it always came back around to magic, but now it feels like I can really get to know about Kiran. Things can finally go back to being peaceful.

But that all depends on Cyra.

What Kiran's mother said to me suddenly flashes in my mind. It occurs to me that I never did figure out what she meant by that. Seath is clearly apprehensive about her, but on the other hand, Kiran and his family work for her and they're kind people.

Time flies as the day goes on, and it feels like it's over far too quickly. After fourth period, Kiran and Cara gather their belongings and converge at my locker.

It's loud in the halls, but that's normal for the final day. Everyone is excited, so it's rowdy.

As Kiran approaches, I suddenly feel a sickening shiver up my spine, and his face scrunches up as well. He looks around with a scowl on his face, then comes to Cara and I.

"Did you feel that?" he says, clearly on guard.

I nod. "I can sense something, but I can't put my finger on it."

"Magic?" Cara asks.

"Yeah, but this is different from anything I've felt before, it's not like with the thralls, this is . . . scary," I say as the eerie feeling runs through my body like static.

Kiran walks past us. "Let's get away from the school for now."

Cara and I follow him, but when we reach the main entrance we find a huge crowd in our way. Kiran taps the shoulder of a random student and asks him "What's going on?"

The boy shrugs. "The doors are blocked, apparently. Nobody can get out."

Kiran turns and heads down the hall, speed-walking toward one of the rear doors, fast enough that Cara and I have to jog to keep up. He reaches the doors and pushes past a small crowd of students to try and force them open, but they won't budge. He comes back to us, dragging Cara and I away from the crowds filling the halls and up to the second level.

A sense of dread fills my chest, and it starts to feel like the walls are closing in around me. Everything in my body screams at me to get out of the school.

"What is it?" I ask.

"Some kind of spell is blocking the doors. Come on," he says, leading us down the hall. "Let's try a window."

I activate Celly from my pocket and let them out. Kiran leads us to the first classroom he can find and tries to open the windows, but he can't.

"Enough of this," he growls, taking his grimoire out of his bag, and raising his hand. He casts a concussive blast at the window creating a shockwave that launches the nearby desks in the opposite direction, but the window remains unscathed.

He fires several more spells; firebolts, lightning, shockwaves, he even summons his flame sword and wails on it repeatedly, but he doesn't make a dent.

Finally, he relents, stepping back from the window.

"Something's weird," Cara says suddenly, looking back at the door. "We're making a lot of noise, but no teachers have come to see what's going on."

"There's no noise at all," I add, frowning. "With everyone downstairs trying to get out it was crazy loud in here, but I just realized it's gotten super quiet."

Cara takes her bow and quiver out. "You should change, too," she says.

Kiran steps out of the room and into the hallway while I change into my witch clothes, then Cara and I join him.

We head back downstairs, and sure enough, the crowds are all still there. But something is wrong.

"They're all frozen," Cara points out.

It's true. No one is moving, talking, or even breathing. It's like they're all statues. Celly flies up from my pocket, and their avatar stares at the students.

Cara reaches out to one of the students, but as soon as she makes contact, they start to melt. Cara and I both shriek in horror as all the students melt away like hot wax into puddles and evaporate.

"What's happening?" I scream.

"I detect that we are trapped in some kind of magical space," Celly says.

"A subspace," Kiran whispers, more to himself. Then; "This is powerful magic. We've been sealed off from reality, probably to separate us from all the regular people," Kiran explains as he inspects the walls. "There must be a way out, come on!"

We run through the school, trying every door we can find, until we burst into the gym. As we enter, the doors slam shut behind us, and Kiran throws himself against it trying to pry it open.

Giving up, he kicks it in frustration.

Our gym doubles as an auditorium. There is a stage on the far side, its scarlet curtains hanging open.

"There's another exit behind the stage," I say, and I lead our group across the gym.

As I reach the middle, something draws my attention to the high windows near the ceiling. One suddenly bursts inward, and the eagle swoops in.

It flies around the gym as we all watch, and as it soars over the stage it sheds a single feather.

The feather drifts lazily to the floor. It rests for a brief moment, then explodes into a dramatic globe of fire. The heat radiating from the stage is scalding and the light near-blinding, but I force myself to look, afraid to turn my back to the horrifying presence within. The flames morph into the shape of a woman and disappear.

She is tall and slender, with tight black pants and long black boots. She wears a long, black, sleeveless tailcoat with gold lining, and a black witch's hat with gold trim. Her right arm is covered in a tribal line art tattoo of various beasts from shoulder-to-wrist, and upon her right hand, adorned with three gold rings with different gemstones, is the same Sigil that Kiran has.

The woman glares at me with her golden eyes, and she brushes her wild mane of black curly hair from her face.

"Cyra Oralie," I whisper.

The Witch of the Sun.

XVI.
The Witch of the Sun

Cyra Oralie's presence is immense and intimidating. Her gaze feels petrifying, and her magical aura seems to swallow all of us whole. I am left feeling paralyzed.

"I am the Witch of the Sun, and leader of the Golden Coven. I have been watching you, Selena Amaris, Witch of the Crescent Moon," her powerful voice booms.

"Mistress Oralie, I–" But Kiran's voice is cut off by a strangled holler of pain as he is dragged to his hands and knees by some powerful, oppressive force.

"You're hurting him!" I shout. "Please, let him go!"

I can sense the invisible weight from Kiran's back disappear, and he is left wheezing, struggling to catch his breath.

"What do you want?" Cara demands.

"It's simple. You have used your magic recklessly, and you have declared yourself heir to a dangerous power. You are not fit to be a witch, and I cannot allow you to follow in the footsteps of your predecessor. You will surrender your sigil to me and you and your friend will forget everything about the existence of magic."

"You can't do that," I plead. "I worked hard to learn about magic and become a witch! Please, don't take my powers."

"If there are any rules we have violated, we were unaware," Celly adds.

"This is not a debate!" Cyra roars. "You will give up your magic now, or I will break you."

Tears form in my eyes. "I'm sorry for whatever I've done wrong, but please! You don't have to do this, I can learn to do better! You can teach me!"

Cyra raises her hand, and my entire body erupts in agony. I scream until my throat hurts, and all the strength in my body disappears in an instant. I collapse to the ground and writhe as flames engulf every inch of me.

"This fire will not physically hurt you," Cyra shouts over my screams. "It will simply inflict this pain, for as long as I will it. I can leave you to endure this agony for months, until you succumb to madness. I can let you scream until you physically cannot produce the sound. Is that what you want?"

"Selena!" I can hear Cara shout, but from the corner of my eye, I can see her collapse and struggle to breathe for almost a full minute.

The pain is so intense that I can't think or focus. I can barely hear over my own screaming, and it robs me of all control over my body.

Just when I feel like I can't take anymore, there is a loud smash, and the pain ceases.

I wipe my eyes and look back at the door we entered through to find it has been kicked right off its hinges. Seath walks in with his ice-claws formed over his hands.

"Seath!" I croak. Kiran comes up behind me to pull me to my feet.

Cyra scowls. "So Yukiko's mad dog finally shows himself. You've aged."

A sudden array of ice spikes appear around Cyra and launch at her to impale her, but a shockwave of flame destroys them all. Seath runs across the gym and jumps at her, swiping with his claws, but they snap off and break against an invisible wall.

"Go!" he commands. "All of you! I'll hold her off. Get back to the mansion!"

Before I can speak, a ball of wind appears around Kiran, Cara, Celly, and I, just as an explosion goes off. The heat and shockwave impacts on the wind harmlessly.

"Run!" Seath shouts.

"Come on," I say, helping Cara up. Kiran leads as we all escape the gym. Just before I leave through the ruined door, I see Seath thrown back. He stays on his feet and uses his claws to block a blast of fire, then charges at Cyra again.

We flee toward the front doors, finding them unlocked.

But when we pass through, we come out in a hallway on the second floor.

"What's going on," Cara cries. "We can't escape?"

194

"She's warping space to keep us trapped!" Kiran says. "But if Seath can get in, there must be a way out. Come on!"

We try door after door, but each one just leads us to a different classroom or hallway. None of them lead out, and with every door we encounter, my fear and panic gets worse.

Finally, we throw ourselves through the back door, and wind up back in the gym. The door Seath destroyed is intact again, and when we turn back it's gone—leaving only a solid wall in its place.

"Oh no," Cara gasps.

I follow her gaze to the wall opposite the stage. Seath is bound in red-hot chains, suspending him in the air by his arms, each being pulled in a different direction. He is battered and bruised, and his ice claws are completely shattered. Cyra stands at the base of the stage, unharmed.

Kiran summons his flame sword and charges at her.

Cyra waves her hand in his direction, and his sword disappears and he falls to his knees in pain, clutching his right arm and wailing. His sigil is burned away from his skin, rendering him powerless.

"Did you seriously think I would let you challenge me with my own power? You are my vassal no longer, you treasonous wretch," Cyra bellows and sends a concussive blast into his chest. The shockwave launches him into the wall, and he collapses, unconscious.

"Kiran!" I cry out.

Cara grimaces and begins firing arrow after arrow at Cyra, with each one burning to ash and dissolving harmlessly before they hit her. "You can't just keep hurting people!" she cries.

Cyra raises her hand and Cara's bow bursts into flames, forcing her to drop it. She is levitated several feet in the air before being launched at high speed into the wall opposite Kiran. She crashes into it and collapses on the ground.

The panic begins to set in, and I suddenly find it difficult to control my breathing. The mere sight of Cyra fills me with terror, and my knees are on the verge of buckling in fear. I have to get out. I have to get away from here.

"Let us out!" I scream, and as I do a shockwave erupts from my body and creates massive tears in the floor and walls and ceiling.

Looking around, I finally understand. This school is a box she is using to trap us. No matter where we run in the box, we cannot escape, but we can destroy the walls of the box itself.

I concentrate, feeling my magic gathering in my hands. I throw my branded hand to the sky with a mighty roar and release a second shockwave that completely destroys the school.

We are instantly transported to the track field. The sun bears down on us, uncomfortably bright and hot. Seath's chains are broken and he collapses to the ground, unconscious.

Celly hovers at my shoulder as I stare down Cyra.

"Based on the difference in experience and technical skill, I don't believe you can win this fight" they say.

I look around at my friends, then back to Cyra, who smirks at me. "I know."

XXVII.
Elatha Yukiko

I think back to all the magical skills I've learned up to this point, and I try to combine them all to defeat Cyra.

Celly casts a barrage of lightning strikes from above while I try to force the grass to rapidly grow into tendrils to restrain her. She sends out a wave of fire killing all of the grass and creates mirror-like surfaces at random that intercept the lightning and send it arcing back toward me.

As I dodge the lightning, I generate countless ice stalagmites, but she destroys them all with a burst of flame.

I summon Kiran's fire blade in my right hand and the lightning blade in my left, and I run at Cyra. I swing both blades one after another, but she dismisses them from my hands and hits me with a concussive blast to my stomach, throwing me far back and sending me crashing into the ground.

She knows more about magic than I ever will. My only hope is to hit her with everything I have and hope that's enough to shake her.

I drag myself back up and send a concentrated bolt of air at her, but it hits her with no effect. I then use my sigil to copy and cast the bat's soundwave attack through Celly's speaker, while at the same time summoning a windstorm to batter her, and yet our barrage appears to have no effect. She stands, completely unharmed, like some impenetrable demon.

Still, there must be some way to overcome her. She can't be invincible.

She raises her sigil hand to me, and suddenly every part of my body feels like it weighs a thousand pounds. The weight drags me down to my knees despite my struggling, and no matter how hard I try, I can't stand.

"You really don't understand a single thing," Cyra mocks. "Do you know why your magic can't harm me, no matter how hard you try?"

Celly flies over to her and blasts her with flame, but she backhands them and sends them tumbling toward Cara's unconscious form.

"The moon provides no light of its own, all it can do is reflect the light of the sun," Cyra explains. "Your magic is only a cheap reflection of my own. Just as the moon may never surpass the sun, the Witch of the Crescent Moon will never be able to surpass the Witch of the Sun."

Maybe she's right, but I don't have to surpass her. I just have to protect my friends.

I focus my attention to the sky and several stars appear despite the overwhelming light pollution from the sun, and lasers rain down from those stars at Cyra. They catch her off-guard, and as they hit her, they start to encase her whole body in ice.

Cyra's body erupts in a powerful flame, and the light of the sun grows infinitely more intense, blocking out the stars and ceasing their barrage.

She glares at me, and I feel pure rage from her golden eyes.

"Stubborn child! I cast your moon into darkness!" she declares.

The sun begins to set, retreating over the horizon until it disappears entirely.

And the moon does not rise. The stars do not appear. The sky is just . . . empty.

It is infinitely dark. So dark that I can't even see my hands when I hold them up by my face. I create a fairy light, but the darkness swallows it in an instant. Every flame I generate is blown out moments later. I stumble around in the pitch blackness, but I cannot feel anything except the cold ground.

"Hello?" I call. There is no answer.

The dark is oppressive and suffocating. I feel like I can't breathe.

"Seath?"

I try to run for as long as I can before I get tired, but I keep tripping over my own feet, and no matter how far I go, I can't get out.

"Kiran?"

A growing anxiety forms in my chest. It's so quiet that I can hear my heart thumping, and it makes me more nervous.

"Celly?"

Where is everyone? Where am I? Is this another subspace? Is this some kind of spell?

"Cara?"

The darkness continues to yield no answers.

"Mom? Dad? Mr. and Mrs. Hoku? Is anyone out there?"

I start to cry. I can feel the darkness not only surrounding me, but penetrating my very being. I sit on the ground and hug my knees, praying for someone, anyone, to find me and save me. The sobs escape my lips, and my eyes start to sting from crying.

I'm scared. I don't know what to do, or how to get out of here.

I just want to go home.

I don't want to lose my powers, and I don't want to forget, but what if Cyra is right? What if there is really nothing I can do to beat her? Giving up could be the only way out of this darkness. It could be the only way back to the others.

I dwell on these thoughts for what feels like days as I sit in the endless void.

The darkness makes me feel small and vulnerable, and yet I have no one I can call to for help. No one is coming.

A name comes to mind, though I know it's a long-shot. But I am desperate enough to call out to anyone, so I resolve to try this person.

If ever you are lost in the darkness, seek the light I have left within you. Her words echo in my head, and I call for her.

"Yukiko?" I croak, my voice hoarse.

I am met by utter silence. Just when I'm about to give up hope, a light appears in the distance.

It is small and difficult to make out, but as it draws closer, I realize it's a lime-green moth, like the one I noticed by Yukiko's grave. Its luminescence pierces the darkness, and I curiously reach my hand out to it. As my finger touches it, it transforms into Yukiko's form, just as I remember her. Her body glows a pale and gentle light. It's easy on my eyes, but the darkness cannot claim it.

"Are you real?" I ask.

Yukiko nods, a gentle smile on her face. "I've been here the whole time, waiting for this moment."

Tears well once more in my eyes. "I let everyone down. Cyra was too strong, I couldn't beat her."

"Everything happened just the way it was always meant to, my moonchild," she coos, kneeling in front of me. "I foresaw that you would come one day, so I created a little mischief with my friends so that you could experiment with your powers and grow as a witch. I knew that one day, Cyra Oralie would come for you, and that you would need me, so I cast this spell over thirty years ago, so that I could guide you in this moment."

"What can I do?" I ask her.

"Close your eyes and sleep, and when you wake, seek me out," she replies.

As her cool, slender hand touches my forehead, I close my eyes and become incredibly drowsy. All my anxiety is replaced with a comforting warmth in my heart, and a feeling of safety that lulls me to sleep.

As I lay my head on the ground and drift away, I hear Yukiko's voice echo in my head.

"Everything will be okay, my moonchild."

My eyes shoot open. It's dark, and I'm covered in a thick blanket in bed. I throw the covers off and sit up slowly, feeling around in the dark for my phone.

"Celly?" I call, but there is no answer.

I look around the room and start to get nervous. This isn't my room. The walls are a cool mint-green, and the bedding matches. There is a desk with books scattered across it beneath the window, and beyond that is a dresser. The nightstand beside this bed has an old-fashioned alarm clock, and there is an open walk-in closet on the opposite wall, with a mirror hanging on the door.

On the bedroom door hangs a calendar. I climb out of bed and approach it, and the horror sets in upon reading the month and year.

December, 1993. *That's thirty years ago.* I look down at my hand and my sigil is gone.

Yukiko's instructions echo in my head.

"Seek me out."

The story will continue in:

Selena's Magica Somnia

Book 2: *The Sun and the Sea*

A.V. Dawn

Scan the QR code below or visit lunarwillow.com to sign up for our monthly newsletter and get access to updates before anyone else, exclusive additional content, behind-the-scenes stuff, and deals. Staying connected helps us to keep creating new and exciting content! We appreciate your support.